Almost Dead

A Murder Mystery

A Novel

By

James J. Murray

ALSO BY JAMES J. MURRAY

Fiction

Lethal Medicine

ALMOST DEAD

A Murder Mystery Novel

Written by
James J. Murray

Published by
Interaction Media Publishing, LLC

ISBN 10: 1530246563
ISBN 13: 9781530246564

First Printing; March 2016
Printed in The United States of America
Revised Edition: August 2016

Dedication

~ For Jean Jackson ~

Without your encouragement and
the support of your ALIR Class,
this book would not have been possible.

Chapter 1

Homicide Detective Rosie Young glanced toward her partner Vince Mendez. She slouched in the passenger seat to shield her eyes from the morning sun. It had been a tough night and she rubbed some tension from her neck as she slid down the seat.

Vince gripped the steering wheel of the department vehicle tighter, yawned and shook his head slightly—an indication of the same weariness that Rosie felt as they drove to the morgue. Both had been up most of the night securing the crime scene.

A woman died of an apparent overdose the previous evening. The circumstances of the event, however, puzzled the uniformed officers who were the first to arrive at the scene. Following procedure, they called in the homicide division.

Irritated at first by the callout for an overdose, Rosie became more intrigued when no drugs were found at the scene and no needle marks were evident with the medical examiner's initial assessment of the body.

She sighed heavily as Vince drove and gave his wrinkled clothing the once-over, a silent amusement she often allowed herself. Tall and lanky, his arms too long and shoulders too narrow, her partner always had the appearance of wearing hand-me-downs, even when sporting freshly pressed shirts.

Looking beyond him and out the driver's side window, she noticed the morning traffic crowding the roadway. She took in a deep breath and focused on the case once again. "Okay, Vince, let's go over what we have. Sandra Dunn, a 30-year old female, drops dead in her apartment—no apparent cause of death. She's alone, wallet still in her purse, the medical examiner is puzzled and emphatically states there'll be no new info without a full autopsy. The ME takes fluid samples, says she'll get back to us on cause of death. The only evidence of possible foul play is that broken window."

"We'll have to locate friends, other family, see if she had any enemies," Vince said. "We should interview her mother again, even though that was tough the first time."

"It's never easy to lose a child, no matter if she was already an adult." Rosie thought back to the first officer on the scene. He reported that he found the mother almost incoherent and standing over the daughter, who was sprawled on the kitchen floor. The mother was muttering something about being invited to dinner.

Rosie turned to Vince. "The mother used her key to enter the apartment when the daughter didn't respond to the doorbell. I'd never give my mother a key to my apartment."

Vince gave a tired shrug. "The mother didn't offer much except that everyone loved her daughter. She seemed distracted to me, like she couldn't focus. You pick up on that?"

"She was sort of a wreck. After all, Vince, she'd just found her daughter dead."

He gave her a thoughtful frown, stroked his chin in that special way he did when not convinced about how the facts lined up in a case. They drove the rest of the way to the morgue in silence.

Detectives Young and Mendez had become partners six months earlier and were still learning to work together without pissing each other off. Rosie was the senior detective—in essence Vince's boss. She had an efficient, almost impatient, aura surrounding her. She dressed the same way every day—starched black jeans and a tank top under a short black leather jacket. The only thing that varied was the color of the tank barely visible under the jacket. Her short hairdo and minimal make-up completed the self-assured look.

They arrived at the Bexar County Medical Examiner's Office, which was located on the sprawling campus of The University of Texas Health Science Center in the heart of San Antonio's north medical center area. Vince parked in the lot adjacent to the morgue and they entered the building. They pushed through the waist high swinging gate next to the reception desk. Each gave the receptionist an exhausted nod as they headed back.

As they strolled down the central hallway, Becky Nolan, the medical examiner on call the previous night, spilled out of the autopsy room door and almost crashed into them. She jumped, started to run toward her office but stopped suddenly and put a hand to her chest. She was hyperventilating. "I was about to call you," she said.

Becky had been an ME for all of three months, but her work on previous cases assured the detectives that Nolan's insight and knowledge of forensic science was flawless. She looked like a teenager, with red hair and freckles, and didn't fit the usual image of an ME; but when she opened her mouth, logic tumbled out in disciplined order.

"You have good news for us about Sandra Dunn?" Vince asked.

Nolan stared at him. "Do I look like I have good news?"

Rosie furrowed her brow. "What's wrong, Becky?"

"I can't find the body, that's what's wrong! It's gone. I took fluid samples from it earlier and undressed her for a preliminary exam, but I had another autopsy to do first before getting to her."

"You're talking about Sandra Dunn, the dead girl from the apartment?" Rosie asked.

"That's the one. She's gone—disappeared! The sheet I had over her? It's in a pile on the floor next to the gurney. I asked every tech if someone moved the body, but no luck. I looked into each cooler drawer. She's not in this building. She's gone!"

"Becky, calm down and think." Rosie walked over, took the ME by the shoulders and looked directly into her eyes. "Dead bodies don't just walk out of the morgue. They're here for a reason."

Getting a look from Becky that could roast marshmallows, Rosie said, "There's got to be a rational explanation. She's been moved somewhere and you simply haven't found the right tech to tell you that."

Becky was about to respond when Rosie's phone rang. She released her grip on the ME and turned to her partner. "Vince, help Becky find the body while I take this."

Rosie stepped to one side of the hallway, leaned against the wall and answered her phone. Vince went down the hall arm in arm with Becky trying to assure her that she wasn't crazy. He verbalized a mental list of all the places a body could get stashed in a morgue, and one by one the ME confirmed that she'd already looked there.

Finally, Becky put her hands up as if she were being robbed. "Enough! I've looked everywhere. I'm telling you, Vince, she's not in the building."

Rosie walked up at that point and put a hand on one hip. "You're right. Sandra Dunn's not in the building."

Vince whirled around and tilted his head to one side. "Not you too? You're saying that body walked out of here?"

Rosie shook her head and a frown creased her forehead. "Maybe so." She turned to Becky and stared at her for a moment. "Are you sure Ms. Dunn was dead when you brought her in?"

"What kind of question is that? No pulse, cool body, no breath sounds—I'm telling you, she was dead." The ME noticed the doubt on Rosie's face.

"Why are you asking me that? I know dead when I see dead!"

"Well, your victim called her mother a couple of hours ago and asked when she was coming to dinner. That call I took was from the mother, and she's mad as hell at us for saying her daughter was dead. When I asked her what she was talking about, she told me she was at her daughter's apartment and Sandra was sitting in a chair next to her—and very much alive."

"That's impossible," Becky blurted out. "I took fluids. Her veins were flat." Becky appeared to be picturing the scene in her mind. "I checked all the vitals. Pupils were fixed. She was cold to the touch."

"But earlier you said she was cool, not cold," corrected Vince. "And you didn't cut into her. You mentioned that you just took blood and urine." He crossed his arms and lowered his chin. "Could she have been in a coma, like in a drug overdose?"

"No, impossible . . . well . . . not impossible." The ME touched the palm of one shaky hand to her forehead. "I was about to perform the autopsy, but the chief wants the autopsies done in a first in first out order. I had one left before getting to her." She looked at Rosie and clenched her hands. "I didn't have time to cut into her. I had to do the other first." The shaky hand went to her mouth, but her muted words were audible nevertheless. "I could have cut into her. I thought she was dead . . . all the signs were . . . I could have killed her!"

Becky seemed to collapse into Vince's arms. He helped her to a bench that was placed against a bare wall in the hall near her office door and gently sat her down. He looked over at his partner. "What do we do now? And what kind of paperwork happens for this? I don't know of any resurrection forms to cover this."

Rosie waited until a curious lab tech walked past them. The tech gave Becky, who was slouched on the hallway bench, a confused look as he walked by.

"We go to Ms. Dunn's apartment," Rosie said. "I told the mother that we'd be there in thirty minutes. We've got to get this smoothed over somehow, but first we need a statement from the victim. We have to establish why she walked out of here without telling anyone."

"What do I tell my boss?" Becky asked in a barely audible voice. "I'll be laughed right out of here, possibly fired over this."

"That's your problem, Becky. Right now we've got a homicide victim to interview." Rosie looked over at her partner and grinned. "Never thought I'd ever say *those* words. Come on, let's go get yelled at by one very angry mother."

Vince followed Rosie down the hall toward the reception area, but he briefly looked back. A very meek Becky was slumped on the bench, looking as if she didn't have the energy to breathe much less move.

Detectives Young and Mendez walked out of the elevator and checked the building's layout.

Apartment 3B was to the left according to the fire code schematic. They arrived at the door and Rosie looked toward her partner before straightening her shoulders. "Okay, Vince, this should be interesting." She pressed the doorbell, heard a dainty chime in response.

Almost a full minute later the door opened and a fiftyish woman with puffy eyes stood before them. She put one fist against a matronly hip and nodded, looking disgusted as she gazed from one detective to the other. "You've come to visit your corpse?" Her lower lip trembled for a brief moment. "How could such a thing happen?"

Rosie put on the best smile she could extract at the moment. "I can't tell you how sorry we are for what we've put you through. Last night when we were here, your daughter appeared to be dead. The medical examiner even confirmed that."

"Well, she's very much alive now." The mom reached up to tuck in a loose strand of blond hair. "I thought I'd lost my baby." Her lower lip trembled again, but she shrugged it off. "So don't just stand there. Come on in and explain all this to us."

The detectives walked timidly into a living room that had an impressive view of the city's downtown area from the wall of glass opposite the couch. Sandra—a younger, thinner, taller version of her mother—was sitting in one of two wing-backed chairs arranged in front of the glass wall.

She stood in a fluid, mannered movement when the detectives entered. "I'm Sandra. I understand I died last night." She spread her hands outward from her waist. "As you can see, I've recovered."

She gestured for them to sit on the couch and took her seat in the chair again. "Detectives, what happened to me yesterday?"

"You don't remember?" Vince asked.

When Sandra lifted her shoulders and shook her head, he asked for more. "What did you think when you woke up in the morgue? And how did you get home?"

"I don't remember any of that."

Rosie raised her hand as if to stop her. "So you're telling me you don't remember waking up in the morgue or how you got here this morning?" When Sandra shook her head, Rosie summoned that forced smile again. "Let's start with what you do know. What's the last thing you recall about last night?"

The mother chimed in. "Honestly, Detective, are you playing twenty questions? She just told you she remembers nothing. I've already asked the same questions a dozen times."

"Mother, please. The detectives need me to answer their questions."

Her mother raised an eyebrow toward her daughter before whirling around and pointing to Rosie. "You told me you had come from the morgue. What did they say? How could they not know my Sandy was alive?"

"Mrs. Dunn, we realize a big mistake has been made. We don't have all the answers right now and this is very confusing for all of us, but I promise we'll get to the bottom of it soon. What I need for you to do is be patient and let me ask your daughter some questions. Is that okay?"

"It's Ms. Dunn. I . . . I don't have a husband at present. You can call me Dolores if you wish."

Rosie forced a smile and turned to Sandra Dunn. "So let me ask again. What do you remember about last night?"

Sandra looked around the room, as if searching for a lost memory. She pursed her lips, tucked a wayward strand of hair into place—an apparent affectation shared with her mother—and gazed toward the kitchen. Both detectives noted the gesture and glanced at each other. Rosie saw that only Sandra's chocolate-colored eyes differed from the mother's pale blue.

The living room encompassed a large open area that included a dining room and a generous kitchen, separated by a serving bar. Dolores sat on a stool at the serving bar as her daughter spoke. "I remember thinking that I should start dinner. I had invited my mother for a visit and promised to cook for her."

As if on cue, Dolores jumped up, went to the kitchen and came out clutching a glass of water. She handed it to Sandra and offered a scowl to the detectives. "Sandy and I are close. We make sure to get together every other week to catch up on things. Sandy said she had to stay late at the office, but last night was the only one she had free. She said she'd call when she got home and I could pop over for dinner."

"Mom only lives a few miles from here," Sandra interjected.

"But I didn't get her call," the mom continued. "I waited a couple of hours before starting to worry.

I tried to phone her, but it went to voicemail. I was concerned so I jumped in the car and drove over." She turned to her daughter, smiled weakly and reached over to give her a hug. "I didn't get a response when I rang the bell. I knocked and still got no response, so I used my key to let myself in. That's when . . . when I found her. I eventually dialed 911 and an officer arrived at the same time as EMS."

"What do you mean that you 'eventually dialed 911'?" Vince asked Dolores.

"I was so distraught when I saw Sandy passed out on the floor. I fumbled in my purse for my phone. I couldn't find it at first. When I finally found it, I was so upset that I dropped it twice while dialing. I took a minute to collect myself, drew in a deep breath and finally got my wits about me." She wiped away a tear that was trailing down one cheek, smoothed the moisture over her manicured hand. "I tried to wake her, but I never learned CPR. I felt so helpless."

"Did you notice the broken window over the sink?" Rosie asked.

"No, not until the officer pointed it out to me. I was focused on Sandy. She looked so . . . pale, so lifeless. I didn't know what to do."

Rosie turned to the victim. "So, Ms. Dunn, you don't remember anything about last night?"

"No, nothing. Mom told me all about what she saw and that they took me away, but I remember nothing."

"Do you recall how you got back to your apartment?" Rosie asked.

"No, I only remember being here," Sandra said and gestured toward the rest of the room.

Rosie looked at the dress the victim was wearing and turned to her mother. "Is that what Sandra was wearing when you found her last night?"

"I think so, but I can't be sure. It was definitely a blue dress."

"But not this blue dress!" Sandra said. Her face showed the alarm she must have felt as she realized that her clothes had been switched.

"So you had on a different dress? What else do you remember about last night? Take a moment to think, Ms. Dunn," Vince said.

"Please, call me Sandy." She looked down at the dress once more and the chair she was in. She clutched the chair arms. "I remember sitting in this chair, in a similar blue dress—but not this one—and thinking that I needed to start dinner. That was when Mom opened the door and walked in."

"That was last night?" Vince asked.

"No, that was this morning. I remember thinking how bright it was outside, but it didn't actually register in my mind why there was daylight until Mom explained that it was morning."

Sandy's mother pointed a finger at the detectives. "What you've put me through—I'll never get over this!" She took a deep breath, turned to Sandy and said more gently, "And to think what my poor baby's been through . . ."

Rosie raised a hand to calm Dolores and turned back to Sandy. "What happened next?"

"Mom screamed when she saw me sitting here. I didn't understand why she was so upset until she told me about last night."

"Sandy was so confused. She couldn't understand why I was so emotional and why I kept hugging her. I'm sure she'll be permanently scarred with the memory of that moment."

"Actually, I almost laughed when Mom said that I died and was sent to the morgue, at least until I realized she wasn't joking." Sandy looked down at her clothing. "I didn't notice that I was in a different dress."

Vince stroked his chin, a sign that something didn't add up to him. He frowned at the mother. "What were you doing here this morning?"

"I came here because . . ." Her voice trembled as she spoke. She put a hand to her mouth to steady her quivering lip and continued. "I called the undertaker. He said they wouldn't release Sandy until after the autopsy, but that I needed to choose something nice for her to wear at . . ." She fanned her face with a hand, wiped moisture dripping down one cheek. "At the funeral."

Rosie stood and walked behind the couch. "Sandra . . . Sandy, is that the first thing you remember, sitting here this morning and thinking about making dinner?"

"Yes, it's as if the last twelve hours have been zapped from my mind. I remember thinking about getting up to make dinner, both last night and again this morning." Sandy shook her head as if she didn't quite believe her own words. "It's so weird. It's like a memory in stereo."

Sandy wrapped her arms around herself as she turned to Rosie. "I'm so scared, Detective. I don't understand what's happened to me. Did I have a psychotic episode? Am I going crazy? Or maybe I have an illness. If so, will this happen again?"

Rosie remained silent and pensive, as if she were about to choose the best answer on a multiple-choice test—only there was no "all of the above" as one of the choices.

Vince looked at his partner and saw her perplexed look. He glanced at the mother and next toward Sandy. "We don't have those answers yet, but I promise you we'll get to the bottom of this. The medical examiner took some of your blood last night. The test results might give us a clue."

"Is that where this bruise came from?" Sandy slid up the sleeve of her dress to reveal a spot on the inside of her left arm. It was a purple discoloration with yellow edges. "My arm hurt this morning and that's when I discovered this strange bruise. I also have a pain and a bruise on my lower abdomen, like someone punched me there."

Rosie remembered that the medical examiner took a urine sample from the body, and probably not nearly as gentle as normal since the victim was presumed dead.

Looking toward the mother, Rosie suggested, "It might be best if we take your daughter to a hospital and have her completely checked out." Turning to the victim, she asked, "Is that okay with you, Sandy? It's inconvenient, but I know you want answers. We all do, and I think it's the best plan of action. We can arrange for you to be transported and admitted immediately, and I'd also like some crime scene techs to go over your apartment again."

Sandy gazed toward her mother for approval, who only nodded in a resigned manner. Sandy said, "Okay, that sounds like a good plan."

Chapter 2

The next morning the detectives went to the hospital to check on Sandy and to get answers in a case filled with nothing but questions. They stopped at the front desk in the busy lobby, flashed their ID badges to an elderly volunteer and waited patiently while the volunteer slowly and meticulously produced visitor passes. She smiled and asked if they needed directions to the elevators. Rosie declined.

She and Vince rode the elevator to the fifth floor and, after announcing themselves at the nurses' station, were directed to Sandy's room.

As they entered Room 505, a private room made more cheerful by a huge bouquet of flowers arranged near the window, the detectives were happy to see that the patient's doctor was in the room.

Dr. Frank Stranton, a tall scholarly looking man with a shock of white hair, turned to them. "I'll just be a minute more. After I finish, you can visit with your friend. If you could wait outside . . ."

Young touched her partner's arm to stop him and she stood in place. "Doctor, we're police detectives. Sandy was a victim of some sort of medical event a couple of days ago. We thought she had died, but now she's very much alive. We'd like to understand how that happened."

The doctor turned, tilted his head and seemed to study Rosie Young from head to toe. He pushed his glasses higher up on his nose with a single finger and glanced over to Vince Mendez before turning back to Sandy. "Any problem with me discussing your case with the police?"

"None, but I hope you can give them better answers than you gave me." Sandy focused on the detectives. "This kind man is my attending physician while I'm here in the hospital. I'm having trouble keeping all my specialist doctors straight so Dr. Stranton is gathering their results, reviewing and interpreting them for me." She looked back toward the doctor and furrowed her brow. "He was giving me some good news, at least I think it's good."

"That doesn't sound promising. Would you care to explain, Doctor?" Rosie asked.

Dr. Stranton drew in a deep breath and gestured to the chart still in his hand. "There really isn't much to tell. Sandy is about as normal as anyone. No brain dysfunction and no abnormalities that I can find. The head scans are unremarkable and the same goes for tests on the rest of her. I'm an internal medicine guy, but the specialists are as puzzled as I am." He sighed heavily and air whistled slightly as it rushed out of his hairy nostrils.

"You found nothing wrong? No abnormal anything?" Vince asked.

Dr. Stranton grinned. "No, Detective . . . no abnormal anything." He turned to Rosie. "Sandy's been checked out from head to toe, and no one can explain why she appeared dead but looks the picture of health now."

"What about the lab results?" Vince asked.

"Her blood and urine tests are fine. Nothing's out of whack. A spinal tap revealed nothing remarkable. The tox screen isn't back yet, however. Maybe it'll give us a clue how to explain this . . . this event."

At that point, Rosie's phone rang and she excused herself to answer it. Dr. Stranton took the opportunity to end the consult. He told Sandy that he would be back when he had more to report. He shook Vince's hand and nodded to Rosie as he left the room. His white coat trailed behind him, the bottom edges flapping as he turned down the hall.

While Rosie was on the phone, Vince pulled out a pair of scrubs, much like the ones Dr. Stranton was wearing under his white coat. They were sealed in an evidence bag that he held up for Sandy to see. "These surgical scrubs were found stuffed into your kitchen garbage container. Do you know anything about that?"

Sandy puffed out her lower lip and shook her head in the negative. "I've never seen those before. They were in my kitchen garbage?"

"They've been identified as the kind issued to personnel at the morgue. Could you have put these on before leaving there?"

"I don't think so." She looked over at the flower arrangement sent earlier by her mom and tried to recall a memory that didn't seem to exist. With a strained voice, she asked, "Why didn't I leave with the dress I had on?"

Vince gave a non-committal shrug, not willing to confirm that the medical examiner had undressed her prior to drawing fluid samples, probably even cutting the dress off of her.

He noticed that his partner grew agitated during the phone conversation. After she hung up, he asked, "Everything okay?"

Rosie smirked and did a slight side-to-side headshake. "Vince, why don't we let Sandy get some rest?" She turned to the patient. "We'll check back when the tox screen results are back. Be sure to give us a call if you need anything."

"I feel fine, Detective. Why can't I go home now?"

Rosie pressed her lips together, briefly looked up at the ceiling before pasting a smile on her face. "You can go whenever the doctors say you can leave. We've got to go now." She nodded for her partner to follow her into the hallway.

When they were fully out of the room, Rosie shut the door. She turned to her partner, who gave her a brief report on Sandy's reaction to the scrubs in the trash. The look on Rosie's face made him ask, "What's wrong?"

"We have another victim."

"A homicide? Okay, let's go."

She put the back of her hand against her partner's shoulder, stopping his forward motion. "I said we have another victim, Vince. It's another one like Sandy."

"What? Someone else woke up from the dead?"

"I don't know the whole story yet, but 911 got a frantic call from a funeral home director a couple of hours ago. He said that when he went to prepare a body, it was gone. The sheets were on the floor. The corpse was nowhere to be found."

"So what happened?"

"Officers were sent to investigate. They arrived on the scene, checked it out and took a statement from the undertaker. He had little to offer, other than that the person appeared dead and had been sent from the morgue. Said when he got to the funeral home this morning he went down to the prep room, but the body had disappeared. That's all he knows."

"So how'd we get called?"

"The captain heard about the strange call. He jumped into the middle of it. He instructed uniformed officers to go to the dead person's house to check it out, and guess what?"

"The corpse was up and walking around?"

Rosie smirked. "You're a genius, Vince. The captain said to get our butts over there pronto to interview the walking dead guy. He wants us to confirm if these cases are related. It's an older gentleman this time, though. The officers are with him now and they're waiting for us."

The detectives walked up to the quaint bungalow on a quiet, tree-lined street in Monte Vista, an affluent and historic residential district just north of downtown San Antonio. Rosie rang the doorbell while Vince looked around the front yard. Immaculate flowerbeds indicated homeowners with either too much time on their hands, a hired gardener or a retiree who could use a second hobby.

A uniformed officer answered the door. His nameplate read "Officer Sanchez." He asked, "Detective Young?"

Rosie nodded and glanced over to Vince. "This is my partner Detective Mendez. Who's with you and how's the victim handling this?"

"Officer O'Connor is with me—actually with *him* now—the dead guy. O'Connor's been really good about calming him down."

"Does he realize what happened to him?" Vince asked.

"He didn't at first. The thing is, we walked up to the house to have a look around. O'Connor walked around back and I was about to check the front door lock when Mr. Mason—that's the dead guy . . . *was* the dead guy—anyway, he opened the door and . . . well, he scared the crap out of me."

Rosie stepped toward the officer, rested a hand on his shoulder. "It's okay, just tell us what happened, in the order that it happened. Okay?"

"Sure. Well, Mr. Mason startled me so I drew on him."

Rosie looked down, grinned and bit the corner of her lower lip. "You leveled your weapon on Mr. Mason?"

"He was supposed to be dead!" Officer Sanchez took in an extra helping of fresh air. "I mean, he was there, in front of me, and he'd been a corpse before."

"How did you know he was the guy from the funeral home?"

"The funeral director showed me a picture of the body . . . you know, when he was over there all dead."

Vince stepped up. "Okay, we get it. So what did you do next?"

"Mr. Mason screamed . . . and I sort of screamed. That's when I realized I was still aiming my weapon at him. I holstered my gun and about that time O'Connor came running from around back."

Rosie suppressed a chuckle threatening to erupt. "She heard you scream?"

Sanchez averted his gaze but nodded in the affirmative. "I heard O'Connor say, 'What the hell?' while Mr. Mason shouted, 'What's the meaning of this?' and I said something like, 'You're supposed to be dead.'"

"I'm sure Mr. Mason appreciated that comment," Vince said with a grin.

"He wasn't smiling, sir. He sort of staggered back into the entry. I rushed in to catch him. I thought he was going to pass out."

"Did he?"

"No, sir. But he sort of frowned, looked confused. Next he blurted out, 'What? I'm dead?' I told him, 'I don't think so, but could we come in and talk about it?'"

Rosie put a hand to her forehead, felt a headache coming on and rubbed vigorously. "Okay, Sanchez. I think it's time we talk to Mr.

Mason." She moved forward, but the police officer didn't step back. "Sanchez!"

"Oh, sorry. This has me a little . . . unnerved. You should hear all the rest directly from the dead guy . . . or the guy who used to be—"

"Sanchez!"

The office led the detectives through the entry, down a wide hall to the back of the house and into a large living room that overlooked a manicured yard full of ornamental bushes and overflowing flowerbeds. Mr. Mason was sitting in a wingback chair opposite Officer O'Connor, who sat on a curved couch arranged center stage in the room.

"Mr. Mason, I'm Detective Young and this is my partner Detective Mendez."

"Yes, Detective, we've been expecting you. I'm Gerald Mason, but you can call me Gerry. That's Gerry with a G, not a J. Everybody spells it with a J, but that's not me."

Rosie stared for a moment before saying, "We won't make that mistake, Mr. Mason . . . I mean Gerry. Could I ask you, how do you feel?"

"If you mean, do I feel dead, the answer is no. I feel fine, at least I did until these policemen came to my house and told me I had kicked the bucket." He gave a nervous laugh and shook his head. "Clearly, there's been some mistake. As you can see, I'm a bit wrinkled and shop-worn—I'm going to be 76 this month—but I'm very much alive."

"We started to call the paramedics, but Mr. Mason refused medical attention," Sanchez explained.

Rosie and Vince nodded in unison. Rosie asked, "Gerry, did the officers tell you that you were in a funeral home yesterday? You died when your pacemaker failed. You had a complete cardiac arrest. You were about to be embalmed this morning when the undertaker discovered that you were gone."

Mr. Mason looked around the room, touched a hand to his throat and gazed out the glass French doors into the back yard. "Yes, they said about as much, but there's obviously been a mistake. I never left this house yesterday. I've been here all the time."

"Mr. Mason—Gerry—do you live alone?" Vince asked.

"Yes, never married, have lots of friends, though. And I have an art studio out back. I paint, primarily in oils and acrylics. That's where I was yesterday, out there all day until . . ."

"Until when, Gerry?" Rosie asked.

"Well . . . I remember coming into the house to do some correspondence at my desk before fixing dinner." He pointed to a corner of the room that contained an ornate desk-hutch combination that was tucked into the angles of the walls. Art periodicals and some scattered mail were stacked to one side.

"What did you have for dinner, Gerry?"

"That's the confusing part. I haven't had dinner yet. I was still at my desk when these officers started snooping around." He pointed to O'Connor. "I saw her come around the corner of the house near the kitchen. It startled me, so I went to the front door to see what was happening on the street."

"Is that when you saw Officer Sanchez on your front porch?"

"Yes, I opened the door and . . . and I guess I surprised him because he drew his weapon and . . . he *pointed* it at me!"

O'Connor stood, crossed over to Mr. Mason and gave his hand a squeeze. "It's okay, Gerry. We didn't mean to scare you. Simply tell the detectives what happened." She turned to Rosie. "He doesn't seem to remember anything about having a heart attack, being picked up by the wagon, or anything about the funeral home. He didn't even realize that one of the windows in the kitchen had been smashed."

"Officer O'Connor is right. I don't remember anything about those events, and I don't know what happened to that window. The boy next door practices batting. Sometimes the ball ends up in my yard. Maybe he hit a fly that came through my window."

Both detectives focused on O'Connor. She gave Gerry's hand another squeeze before letting go. "We found no ball in the house, but the window was definitely broken from the outside. And Gerry mentioned something about a change in clothes."

"There are a few glass shards on the kitchen countertop," Officer Sanchez said.

"What about his clothes?" Rosie asked O'Connor.

"Gerry remembers what he was wearing after coming in from painting, when he sat down to do correspondence. The pants and shirt he's wearing now are different."

Rosie looked toward Gerry. "How different?"

"Well, they're basically the same color and design, and they're definitely my clothes, but this shirt is a little different than before and it has no paint spots on it. It's not what I was wearing in the studio or when I sat down at my desk. I didn't really notice that until the officers arrived and started questioning me." He touched his temple and smiled. "I become a little forgetful at times, especially when I'm tired after a long painting session. I can only speculate that I spilled paint on me and changed before sitting at my desk."

"Vince, check the trash cans. See if there's any clothing in them."

While Vince looked around the house, Rosie asked, "So, Gerry, what else do you remember about yesterday?"

"I remember sitting at my desk working on correspondence when I saw this policewoman coming around the back of my house. I thought it was yesterday afternoon, but now I know it was this morning—a whole half day later. Jeez, how's that possible? What's happened to me?"

"We don't have those answers yet, but we're working on it," Rosie said.

Vince walked back into the living room holding a medical gown, like one would put on before getting a medical exam. He held it up with a gloved hand. "Found this in the kitchen trash."

"That looks like what the undertaker had hanging on hooks in his embalming room. Is that what Gerry came home in?" Sanchez asked.

Vince and Rosie exchanged glances. Vince instructed Sanchez to bag the gown as evidence.

"I wore that?" Gerry asked as he pointed to the gown. "And how did I get back here . . . with only *that* on?"

Vince stroked his chin and frowned. "Could you tell us exactly what you *do* remember about being at your desk? Can you think back, maybe close your eyes and concentrate, try to remember any details?"

"Okay, I'll try." Gerry took a deep breath, pushed back his shoulders and let his arms fall to his side. "I'd been sitting at my desk for about an hour. As I said, I was in my studio out back earlier, but got tired of painting. I needed to pay some bills, so I sat at my desk and began to organize the mail that had piled up. I gathered several magazines that I'm behind in reading, put them to the side so I'd have room to work. I opened the mail—it was quite a stack, but mostly junk. I threw out a bunch as I sifted through the pile."

"Did you feel ill or feel anything other than normal at the time?" Rosie asked.

"Not that I recall. It was a regular day taking care of a boring chore. But . . ." He frowned, as if trying to remember an important detail.

Vince's face brightened at the prospect of a clue. "But what, Gerry? Did something happen at that point?"

"I think so. I remember something distracted me, maybe a noise, but I don't recall what."

"Was it glass breaking?" Rosie asked.

"I don't know. That probably would have made me jump from the desk, but I didn't. I only turned toward the back yard. I think the noise was maybe a scratching sound."

"Do you have a pet, Gerry, a cat or dog that maybe was making that noise?"

"No animals, I'm all alone." That statement seemed to bother him more than the fact that he had experienced a near fatal event the previous day.

Rosie noticed and walked over to him. "Gerry, something very unusual happened to you yesterday. We need to take you to a hospital to have you checked out. Would you be okay with that?"

The man seemed to crumble into himself. His shoulders slumped forward and he sank deeper into his chair. "I don't like hospitals. People go there to die."

O'Connor smiled at Gerry. "It's okay. It's only precautionary. I'll even ride with you to the hospital if you wish." The officer turned to Rosie to make sure that was acceptable.

"Sure, O'Connor, I think Gerry would like you to go with him."

Vince nodded and plucked his cell phone from his coat pocket. "I'll call the lab, requisition some techs out here to pull prints from that window and to go over the rest of the place. Sanchez, make sure the techs take that gown and have them check for prints on that trash can."

Rosie pulled out her phone as well. "I'll arrange transport to the hospital and let them know what to expect." She glanced over at O'Connor. "You're on hospital duty as of right now."

Chapter 3

After Gerry Mason and Officer O'Connor were transported to the hospital in an ambulance, Rosie and Vince remained behind with Officer Sanchez. Their first priority was to secure Mason into a medical facility and have him examined for possible clues to his apparent resurrection, but Rosie wanted some quick answers from the responding officer remaining with them.

"Sanchez, get over here," Rosie ordered and gestured to a chair.

The officer swallowed hard and quickly took a seat in a chair opposite from where she stood. "Yes, ma'am?"

Rosie paced back and forth in front of him as she spoke. "Okay, Mason was on a slab in a funeral home this morning. He got up, left there and showed up here—all the while thinking he'd never left home. You and O'Connor interviewed the funeral home director. What'd you find?"

"He said a dead guy was missing from his embalming room when he arrived at work this morning. He noticed that a medical gown he had hanging on a hook was also missing. The back door was closed but unlocked. He looked all over the place for the guy before dialing 911."

Rosie stopped pacing, moved closer to the officer and stared down at him. "That's it?"

"There wasn't much else the funeral director could offer. He was pretty unnerved by what had happened, said that he'd never lost a corpse before."

"But, Sanchez, there had to have been transport paperwork on Mason."

Vince mentally constructed a timeline for the victim's last 24 hours and piggybacked on Rosie's statement. "People had to be involved in getting him from home, to the morgue and finally to the funeral home yesterday. Who signed him out of the morgue?"

Sanchez held out his palm and closed his eyes for a moment. "Hold on. I have all that in the patrol car. I'll be right back." The officer jumped up, slid past Rosie and hurried from the room.

While Sanchez went to the cruiser, Vince tilted his head toward Rosie. "Mason was about to be embalmed. Someone had to have authorized that and the funeral."

"But just now—before the paramedics took him to the hospital—Mason said he didn't have any relatives to call."

"Yes, and did you see the look on his face when we asked about close friends? Gerry Mason seemed to have trouble coming up with any names."

Sanchez returned to the living room and opened a folder of assorted documents. He pulled out one page and handed it to Rosie. "Here's the paramedic's report. It states a neighbor came over to bring him leftover cake from her son's birthday party. She knocked, got no response, thought he was out in his studio but couldn't find him there. So she went to the French doors at the back of the house to leave the goodies. She happened to look in, saw him on the floor and called 911."

"It says here that Mason was cool to the touch and they couldn't revive him. It says that his pacemaker wasn't working at the time. Did it malfunction?" Rosie asked.

Sanchez nodded. He handed her a second form from the folder. "That's the story from the morgue. They did a test on the thing. Official cause of death is listed as pacemaker malfunction with resulting fatal heart attack."

"Near fatal," Vince corrected.

Sanchez shrugged, pulled out another piece of paper and handed it to Rosie. "This is a picture of Mason in the morgue. It was sent to the funeral home with the release form. That's how I recognized him when he opened the door—scared the crap out of me, like he was a zombie or something. Only he looked normal . . . I mean, not dead anymore."

"Show me the release form." Sanchez handed Rosie the document. She glanced over it and said, "Someone named Samuel Jennings signed the authorization for the body's release to the funeral home."

"That's right," Sanchez said. "The funeral director told me Jennings was sort of a friend of Mason's and had a Medical Power of Attorney document authorizing him to make medical decisions on behalf of Mason."

"So, with that Power of Attorney document in hand, Jennings could request that Mason be moved from the morgue to the funeral home without an autopsy," Rosie said.

Sanchez nodded. "And Jennings was also planning the funeral."

"So who is Samuel Jennings?" Vince thought out loud. "Has to be a close friend, but why wouldn't Mason want us to call this guy about what happened, or that he was being taken to a hospital just now?"

Sanchez cleared his throat. "Well . . . it seems like Jennings wasn't too fond of Mr. Mason."

"Spit it out, Sanchez," Rosie said.

"The funeral director said all the paperwork was in order, and Jennings didn't seem upset at all. Not like a close friend would be—you know, no tears, no emotion."

Rosie made a circular motion with her index finger indicating that the officer should speed up his explanation. He said, "In fact, Jennings told the funeral home to prepare the body quick and cheap, ordered no viewing time for friends and wanted a simple burial in a plot that he had the deed for." Sanchez pulled out another piece of paper. "This is a copy of the deed to Mr. Mason's burial plot in Mission Park Cemetery."

"So Jennings wanted to get rid of Mason as fast as possible, maybe before any evidence was found," Vince said, stroking his chin and nodding.

"Okay, no speculating, Vince." Rosie looked at Sanchez. "Did you get an address for Samuel Jennings?"

"Sure did. I got a copy of the preliminary bill Jennings was going to have to pay. Has his address, phone and credit card info on it."

Rosie snatched the document out of the officer's hand. "You did good, Sanchez. Now go put up some crime scene tape out front while we wait for the lab techs to arrive." She pulled out her phone and dialed the number on the invoice while Vince went to the broken window to inspect it more closely.

A man answered the call. "Is this Mr. Jennings, Samuel Jennings?" Rosie asked. There was a moment of silence before the man confirmed his identity. "Mr. Jennings, I'm Homicide Detective Rosie Young and I would like to ask you some questions about a friend of yours."

"Homicide? Oh, no. Gerry was murdered?"

"That's what we want to chat with you about. There's been a complication."

"But I thought his pacemaker kicked out on him and his heart stopped. I'm about to bury him. Will that need to be delayed while you investigate?"

"Possibly. I understand you're making the arrangements. Is it okay if my partner and I stop by your place in about fifteen minutes? I see you live close by."

"I'm at work, but you can come here. I have time now." He sighed. "Seems nothing Gerry does stays simple."

"What was that, Mr. Jennings?"

"Nothing, just come on over." He gave Rosie the address to a toy store.

Rosie told Sanchez to wait for the crime scene techs, gathered the documents Sanchez had given her and stuffed them back into the folder. She tucked it under her arm and nodded for Vince to follow. "We're going to visit with Jennings to find out if he's friend or foe."

Vince drove and 45 minutes later they were standing at the counter in a boutique toy store that sold high-end items designed to appeal to overly indulged youths of all ages. Boxed toys were stacked behind clever displays of pricey electronic games, robots, over-sized stuffed animals and educational lab experiment toys.

Samuel Jennings was a grandfatherly looking gentleman. He had no beard but sported a mess of white hair that begged for a Santa hat, and he had the belly to match.

He spoke to one of his two assistants, told him to dust some shelves while there were no customers around, and turned to the detectives. Vince was busy checking out a remote-controlled police car, complete with siren and lights.

Jennings cleared his throat. This got the detectives' attention and Vince placed the car delicately back on its display. Jennings showed them to a small but nicely appointed office. He motioned for them to sit in chairs that faced his desk and offered hot tea. Vince waved off the hospitality, but Rosie said that she'd have a cup.

Jennings took two ornate mugs from a shelf filled with other delicate-looking cups and mugs, poured from a heated carafe and placed a cup in front of Rosie before settling behind his desk.

"I don't have lemon. Will cream and sugar do?"

"Thanks, but straight up is fine. We're here because we have good news for you." She stirred her tea to cool it, waited for a reaction. Getting none, she raised an eyebrow briefly. "Gerry Mason is alive."

"What?" Jennings stood abruptly, so fast that he almost spilled his tea. "That bastard. Can't he even die right and leave me in peace?"

Rosie and Vince frowned and glanced at each other before turning back to Jennings. She said, "Excuse me? We thought that would be welcome news."

"Detective, I gave that man twenty years! He was the love of my life." He looked down at his waist for a moment. "I gained a few pounds and he tossed me out like I was spoiled meat. Finally I thought I was rid of him, but now he comes back? How's that possible? I identified his body!"

Vince scrunched up his chin. "So if you two were no longer together, how is it that you still have Mr. Mason's Power of Attorney?"

"I told him to change all that. I certainly did! I made a new will, cut him out of everything." Jennings looked past the detectives, seemed to focus on thin air. He frowned before turning has attention back to them. In a hushed tone, he said, "You mean he's really alive—walking around and everything?"

Vince nodded and a small grin framed his lips. "Yes, Mr. Jennings, that's what we're saying. We don't have all the answers, but Mr. Mason really didn't die."

"He seemed to have had . . . some sort of episode," Rosie said. "We're investigating."

"That cheapskate—probably still looking for a lawyer who'd change his will for free. Or better yet, he couldn't think of anyone else to list in case of an emergency."

"Was Mr. Mason a difficult person?" Vince asked.

Jennings chuckled and shook his head. "You have no idea. He was so temperamental. The more paintings he sold, the more arrogant he became. It was his way or the highway, a place for everything and everything in its place, the focus always on him. Suddenly I didn't seem to measure up anymore. One day . . ." A long sigh spilled out before he continued. "One day, it was simply over. He told me to get out."

He looked around the office, put a shaky hand to his mouth before waving it in the air around him. "Fortunately, I had this place and could build a future."

Rosie gazed around the office, focused on the wall of books intermingled with vintage toy cars on an expensive-looking bookcase. A side table was topped with an ornate chess set—in all, a tasteful and comfortable use of the small office space. She turned back to Jennings. "You own this place or manage it for someone?"

A look of indignation showed on the man's face. "I own this! Somehow I knew Gerry would get tired of me. I needed something for myself . . . so I could walk away if I chose to."

"Okay, we get the picture." Rosie pushed her tea to the side before changing the subject. "So what happened yesterday? How were you contacted about Mr. Mason?"

"The bastard didn't even have the decency to take me off his phone list. I was still listed as ICE #1 on his cell. So, being his first in case of emergency contact, I got the call that he had died."

"They asked you to go down to the morgue to identify the body?" Vince asked.

"What a repugnant thing that was. They had his ID, and the neighbor had already told the paramedics who he was. Why'd they need me?"

"They must have asked you about family or other friends," Vince said. "Maybe asked who should be contacted about the body?"

Jennings sighed heavily. "Yes, and there's no one for him, no family left—and no one else who'll take responsibility. I went to the house, unlocked his safe—he hadn't even changed the combination or his door locks—and found the Power of Attorney papers. I decided to do this last thing for him and finally be rid of it all."

Vince stroked his chin with an open hand. "Does he have any money, anything you'd inherit? And what about the house?"

"Are you insinuating . . .?"

"We're only gathering facts, Mr. Jennings," Vince assured the man.

"Okay, that's fine. When I was going through the safe, I found his will—the same one he had when we were together. I found no other, so I can only assume he hadn't changed a thing." He looked up at the ceiling, as if reminiscing about something, but continued. "Good for me. I actually *do* get everything. I thought that was kind of him—odd, but kind. And now he's back!" He punched the desk and the mug of tea shook. It remained upright and to Rosie's amazement nothing spilled. "He's going to be so pissed!"

"Why's that?" Rosie asked.

"Well, don't you see? It's one more thing he can blame me for."

Rosie seemed puzzled and looked toward her partner for a moment. Vince asked, "Mr. Jennings, do you feel responsible in some way for Mr. Mason's death? Do you think he'll blame you for what happened to him?"

"No, not his death! But the funeral thing is another story. I got his body released without an autopsy."

"The coroner asked if you wanted one, but you refused. That was your right when the cause of death is obvious. I see no problem here," Rosie said.

"I had him rushed to a funeral home. I was going to get it all done so . . . so *fast*." He ran his thick fingers through his snowy hair. "I just wanted to be rid of him, to finally be done with that part of my life. The cheap funeral . . . no one would have cared."

"You're concerned that he will. He'll be upset with you, won't he?" Vince asked.

"It'll start all over again—the fights, the ridiculing." He sighed again and looked down for a second before focusing back on the detectives. "Is there anything else you need from me? Any reports to sign? Please, don't make me go see him."

Rosie glanced at Vince and nodded toward the door. "No, I think that'll be all for now." The detectives stood and Jennings escorted them to the store's front door, although Vince took a small detour to check out the price on the remote-controlled police car he had played with earlier.

After leaving the toy store, the detectives decided that it was time to check on Gerry Mason. They wanted a preliminary medical report on his health status. Vince drove them to the hospital—the same one Sandy Dunn was in—so they checked on her first before going to Mason's room.

They learned that Dunn had been released from the hospital the previous evening, but that's all the reception desk staff could tell them. They decided to contact her after visiting with Mason. They proceeded to his room on the fifth floor.

As the detectives exited the elevator and walked to the nurses' station, they saw Dr. Stranton, the same hospital physician who had taken care of Dunn, sitting at a workstation typing notes into an electronic charting tablet.

Rosie called out, "Dr. Stranton, could we have a word with you?"

The doctor looked up. He furrowed his brow momentarily before recognition took over. "Detectives, what an interesting day this is. Now it's two walking dead people. If I didn't know better, I'd say we had the beginnings of a zombie invasion. You know, the CDC has a plan for that."

"Yes, but that was a joke, an entertaining campaign on emergency preparedness," Rosie said.

"Well, Ms. Dunn and Mr. Mason are not jokes, just living proof of . . . of a very interesting phenomenon."

"So what's the story here? I understand you let Sandy Dunn go home."

"I had no reason to keep her. The tox screen isn't back yet but she's fine by all medical standards. I had no choice but to respect her wishes to be discharged."

"What about Mr. Mason? Is he fine also?" Vince asked.

Dr. Stranton reflected on his answer for a moment before speaking. "Mr. Mason still has cardiac issues and needs his pacemaker—another one, actually. We're replacing the old one with a newer unit this afternoon. But for an older gentleman, he's as healthy as one could expect."

A nurse excused herself and squeezed past Rosie to head toward a computer terminal farther down the nurses' station. Rosie stepped aside initially to let her pass but then moved closer to Dr. Stranton.

"Why does Mr. Mason need another pacemaker?" Rosie asked.

"The cardiologist doesn't trust the one he has in him. It's a few years old, it stopped on him and caused . . . I don't know, I guess it caused him to die momentarily . . . but it started up again. A diagnostic test of the device indicates it stopped functioning yesterday about five hours before the neighbor called 911. The problem, if you could call it that, is that the device started back up early this morning."

"So this case is different than Ms. Dunn's? It's a faulty pacemaker issue?" Vince asked. He stroked his chin and frowned. "It's likely that Ms. Dunn's case will only open up after her tox screen results are in. But we have a cause of death, so to speak, for Mr. Mason—his pacemaker malfunctioned."

"It's really not as simple as that regarding Mr. Mason, Detective. The pacemaker in him certainly was innovative technology at the time and the FDA still monitors closely all potential malfunctions, but I think *his* pacemaker problem may be secondary to something else."

The doctor scratched his head, looked around the space and considered his words carefully. He noticed that the nurse down the way working at a computer finished her entries and stood. He waited for her to leave the nursing station before turning back to the detectives. "You see, Mr. Mason's pacemaker uses his own heart's motion to power it. So I can't be sure which happened first—the heart stopping the pacemaker or the pacemaker not working and stopping the heart."

Rosie frowned as if she didn't follow what the doctor was inferring. "So what are you saying? You can't explain the malfunction or even that there *was* one?"

Dr. Stranton gave a polite smile and a shrug in return.

Rosie glanced at Vince. He had a perplexed look on his face as well. She turned to Stranton. "Why don't you start at the beginning and walk us through how this device works?"

The doctor nodded and adjusted his chair to face the detectives. "Mr. Mason's pacemaker is really a very simple device. It uses something called piezoelectricity to power it from nanoparticle technology. It creates electricity from piezoelectric particles within the device to drive the machine to regulate Mr. Mason's heartbeat."

Rosie turned to Vince. "Have you ever heard of anything like that?"

"Never," Vince said. He nodded toward the doctor. "Please continue."

"Piezoelectricity is an electrical charge that's generated from motion in the near vicinity of a device that contains these piezoelectric nanoparticles. In Mr. Mason's case, those particles housed in his implanted pacemaker detect the motion of his heart and vibrations from his chest cavity to produce more electrical charges to directly stimulate his heart to pump."

Vince scratched his head. "So you're saying that each time Mr. Mason's pacemaker causes his heart muscle to beat, the beating motion causes an additional charge to power the next pacemaker impulse to create another beat, and that continues on and on?"

"A simplification, but that's exactly what happens," Stranton said. "Only the cardiologists are not sure what happened yesterday regarding Mr. Mason's device. The questions they need answers to are 'Did his heart stop and that stopped the pacemaker from functioning properly?' or 'Did his pacemaker stop working for some reason and that stopped his heart?'"

"So how do you explain that the device suddenly started up again?" Vince asked.

"We can't be sure and it's all speculation at this point, anyway."

When Rosie remained silent and continued her stern stare, Dr. Stranton said, "Okay, the digital readout of the diagnostics on the device shows that the machine stopped functioning, presumably because Mr. Mason's heart stopped beating. But, as the readout indicated, the unit started back up this morning."

"And that's what awakened Mr. Mason?" Vince asked.

"I don't think so. You see, if his heart had stopped because the pacemaker stopped, or vice versa, he would be dead—really dead. But he woke up this morning, from what I don't know, but it certainly wasn't from being almost dead that long."

Vince scrunched up his chin and rubbed the back of his neck. "So you're saying one didn't have anything to do with the other and the pacemaker wasn't to blame?"

Rosie rubbed her forehead and let words flow out of her mouth in a whispered breath. "This is going to be a week to remember." She shifted onto her other foot and looked down at the doctor, who was still seated at the nursing desk. "I'm not sure I understand what you're suggesting."

"What I'm saying is that I think someone jarred the body this morning, or Mr. Mason got up and that caused the pacemaker to kick back on. The problem I'm seeing here is why didn't it happen when he was moved from the morgue? The motion should have been enough to start the pacemaker again, unless the personnel were very gentle with the body."

Rosie removed a file from her large purse and held it up. It contained the documents gathered by Officer Sanchez. "Our report doesn't go into that much detail but it does state that the body went untouched after it got to the funeral home last night."

"That's what I'm saying, Detective. If that's true, then I think Mr. Mason somehow awakened, got off the table and jarred the pacemaker into action at that time. I'm speculating that he . . . that he woke up first."

Vince turned to Rosie and spread his hand out as if holding a platter of food. "So these cases are connected."

"Don't jump to conclusions so quickly, Vince. We're in unchartered territory here." She turned back to Dr. Stranton. "I'd like a copy of the medical workup on Mr. Mason as soon as you have it completed and a copy of his tox screen as soon as it comes in. You *did* do a tox screen, didn't you?"

"Of course. And, yes, I'm as curious about the results as you are. I'll get Mr. Mason's consent to share his medical records with you. Your Officer O'Connor is still here, by the way. She's standing guard at the door. Could you tell her to go home? It's freaking out the staff."

"Okay, we're heading down the hall to see Mr. Mason now. We'll send Officer O'Connor back to the station after we visit with him."

Chapter 4

Vince knocked gently on the hospital room door. Getting no response, he pushed it open only enough to peak in. He sighed and swung the door fully open.

Gerry Mason was sitting in bed, three pillows supporting his back and staring at a TV attached to the opposite wall. He turned toward the door when the detectives entered.

"Mr. Mason, how are you feeling?" Rosie asked.

"Bored out of my mind." He gestured to the TV screen. "How do people watch this stuff? It's all silly games and talk shows about nothing."

Rosie nodded and put on her best smile. "We talked to your doctor and he says you're doing fine, that you have a procedure scheduled for this afternoon to replace your pacemaker."

"Well, they need to get on with it. I'm about to starve to death. I didn't have any breakfast before those officers descended upon me this morning and they won't give me a snack or lunch because I'm having surgery. I might as well be dead!"

Ignoring the man's obvious displeasure, Rosie said, "Apparently, the doctor's are concerned about the pacemaker you have in you."

"That's what Officer O'Connor told me. Thanks for letting her stay. She helped calm me down while all this craziness was going on."

"Since you're in good hands now with the hospital staff, we'll let her go back to her regular job. You'll undergo the procedure soon, have a new pacemaker put in and hopefully have no more health issues."

Mason patted his chest. "That was my understanding when they put this thing into me before. But then I died!"

Rosie bit her lower lip. Vince said, "We spoke with Mr. Jennings earlier."

Mason shot a glance at the detectives and furrowed his brow. "Why get him involved? He has nothing to do with this, or anything else in my life anymore. He's history!"

"That may be so, but thanks to the emergency contact information on your phone, the EMS people were able to contact him and obtain information on you," Vince said.

"It was Mr. Jennings who signed the authorization to have you released to the funeral home," Rosie added.

"What? Who gave him the right to manage me like . . ." Mason stopped mid-sentence, touched fingers to his forehead. "How did anyone know he had the authority to do that? Did that man go through my safe? If he took anything from my house—"

Rosie held out the palm of one hand. "We wouldn't know about that, but Mr. Jennings seems to be a nice person. He knows a lot about your life, knew where to look for your legal documents. He took responsibility for . . ."

Mason gave Rosie a sharp, angry look and finished her statement. "For my remains. You were going to say my remains, weren't you? So what happened to me yesterday? The doctors don't have any answers, but they insist on putting a new pacemaker in me—a different type—and they're charging my insurance a fortune for it."

Rosie gave Mason a sympathetic smile, walked closer to the bed and gave his shoulder a gentle squeeze. "Gerry, we're told it's an appropriate precautionary measure. Your pacemaker stopped for some reason—maybe a malfunction, maybe something else—but why take a chance by keeping something in you that might be faulty?"

"I don't need advice from you, young lady. What I want from you are two things. Keep that tub of lard away from me for starters; and secondly, find out what happened to me. I need to be assured that nothing like this will happen again until it's the real thing."

"The real thing?" Vince asked.

"The next time I die, I plan to stay dead. This waking up after the fact is so confusing. It's disruptive and exhausting, I tell you! And I have an art exhibit opening in two weeks at the Shapiro Gallery. How am I going to get ready for that show now that I'm 'having a procedure'?" He wrinkled his nose and winced as he said those last words.

"The doctors say that replacing your pacemaker is a must," Rosie said.

Mason pointed at her. "Don't tell me what's necessary, young lady. I could lose a week of painting while I recover from a surgery that costs about as much as a year's worth of car payments for that cardiologist."

"Mr. Mason . . . Gerry . . . don't get so worked up," Rosie said as she pasted a false smile on her face and patted his shoulder. "We're trying to get some answers for you. That's our job. Your job is to get back to where you were before all this happened."

Shrugging off Rosie's hand, Mason said, "I'm counting on you for that, Detective—answers, that is—and I want them soon. And Sam Jennings isn't to be involved in any of this, not anymore. Do I make myself clear?"

"Perfectly. We'll leave you for now and start our investigation. We'll be in touch when we know more. Is that okay with you?" Rosie gave Mason's shoulder a final squeeze.

He wrinkled his nose and lifted both shoulders. "Just peachy, Detective. Maybe we can join hands and sing 'Kumbaya' when you come back." His face took on a serious expression as he glanced from Rosie to Vince and back. "Just find out what happened to me. The more I think about it, the more I'm starting to freak out. Now leave. I want to get some rest."

With that dismissal, the detectives left the room, told Officer O'Connor that she was not needed at the hospital any longer and that someone would arrive soon to take her back to the police station to resume her normal duties.

Vince suggested that he and Rosie grab some lunch and try to formulate an investigative attack. They compromised on the lunch venue and chose a café not far from the hospital that offered healthy options in addition to the "greasy spoon" fare that

Vince was so fond of. When they entered the café, most of the tables were filled with the loud, hungry lunch crowd. There was one out-of-the-way empty booth toward the back of the room near the kitchen.

They settled into the large booth, took menus from the gum-chewing waitress and looked over the selections. They ordered food and organized their case files on the large table while they waited for their lunch, each taking a few minutes to review what was already known about Sandy Dunn and Gerry Mason.

When the food arrived, they pushed the files to one side and focused on their meals. Rosie gazed at her veggie burger and frowned at the French fry side order next to Vince's chicken fried steak. He squirted ketchup over the pile of fries, picked up one and guided it to his mouth. A drop of grease mixed with ketchup plopped onto the table.

"I swear, Vince, I don't understand how you stay so skinny."

"Spanx, it's my salvation." When Rosie let out a chuckle, he said, "Now will you lay off my diet? I don't cook at home like you do. I have to get my calories from somewhere."

"So when you get home, you don't eat?"

"Sure I do. I grab a cold beer and a bag of salted nuts. They're loaded with protein, you know."

"Also loaded with fat. Never mind the salt you just mentioned."

He raised an eyebrow, threw an exasperated glare her way. "Just dig into your multi-grain whatever and have a Zen moment. I'll have my moment when I dip a fry into this cream gravy. That's when all will be right with the world."

"Oh, really? We have two dead people who didn't stay dead. I don't know about you, but I don't think my world will ever be the same again."

Vince pinched a fry between his thumb and forefinger. A drop of grease was set free, this time sliding down the palm of his hand. "I hear you. I'm just not sure how to approach these cases. They have to be linked, but the victims are as different as night and day."

Rosie nodded. She chewed and swallowed a bite of burger. "We have to find a starting point and so far I don't see one. On the one hand, we have a young female victim who's cooperative, polite and seems willing to help in any way to get to the bottom of this. Then we have Mason—temperamental, self-centered, a loner and set in his ways."

Vince wiped his hand, picked up a fry and pointed it at Rosie. She flinched like he had pointed a weapon at her. He said, "There has to be a commonality somewhere that links them together. I think that's the starting point—find the link and we find answers."

Rosie took another bite of burger, washed it down with flavored iced tea. "I think we should split up."

Vince looked down at his plate. "Over my diet?"

"No, you idiot. We should divide up our investigation. You talk to Mason's neighbors and the gallery owner where his art show was being held. After that, go back to Samuel Jennings. He seems to know Mason as well as anyone and might fill in some blanks about the man's life."

"And you'll do the same with Sandy Dunn's associates?" Vince asked.

"That's right. Let's take the afternoon to put a profile together on these two victims. We'll meet up in the morning and compare notes. That sound like a plan?"

"About as good as any at this point," Vince said. He picked up the bottle of ketchup, turned it upside down and squirted another glob over his greasy fries.

Chapter 5

The next morning, Rosie sauntered into the squad room holding a cup of Chai Black Tea and a half eaten bran muffin. As she walked up to her desk, she threw the remains of the muffin into the trash and took a sip of tea.

Vince was already at his desk, a greasy egg muffin wrapper off to one side. The large cup of coffee sitting atop the wrapper sent swirls of steam into the air.

"Vince, really? It's a wonder your heart can still pump blood."

"After this morning's 10-miler, my heart is pumping just fine. And don't start already with my food choices. I haven't had enough coffee yet."

She slumped into her chair, opened her large handbag and pulled out a case file. She dumped it onto her desk. She looked around the open area beyond their workspace. Few detectives were in yet and the squad room was quiet. She knew it would remain that way for only another hour or so before there'd be the constant buzz of investigative activity.

"Okay, Vince, you or me first?"

"Rank has its privileges." He spread his hands outward in an inviting gesture.

Rosie drew in a cleansing breath, let it out slowly and opened the file. "Our Ms. Congeniality has an interesting reputation."

"About what?" He shoved his hands under his chin, elbows on the desk.

"I pegged her as a corporate lawyer but she's criminal defense. Her clients are mostly small potatoes. They range from DWI's to drug possession cases and even molestations—the kind of 'she said, he said' stuff that gets messy real fast. She's in a sole practice, her office in a nicely remodeled older home on Broadway and she has a staff of three. There's a receptionist-office manager, an investigator and a paralegal that says she does all the background law research on Dunn's cases. The staff seem close to her, more like friends than professional associates, and they all knew about what happened to her."

Vince shrugged, swirled the coffee in his cup and blew the steam away. "Sounds like an efficient operation. Something I'd expect from Sandy. Everything put together well, sort of like her."

Rosie glanced at him, raised an eyebrow and gave a smirk. He corrected. "Composed, polished I mean."

"That's my impression too, about her *and* her life. She manages a busy schedule with lots of cases. I went to the courthouse, did a trial docket search on her—found nothing high profile. She's well known and people like her, has a reputation as being fair and sensible when dealing with both clients and prosecutors. I talked to several judges who presided over her cases. They pretty much said the same thing."

Vince characteristically rubbed his chin, looked up and to the side. "Hmm, anyone want to know why you were asking so many questions about a lawyer?"

"I said I was investigating a case that she'd be representing. That shut down any personal questions because of the whole attorney-client privilege thing."

"So none of her cases caught your eye?"

"Nothing, so I talked to her neighbors from a list her staff provided. The neighbors say she's friendly and always pleasant, but they didn't seem to know her that well, like she didn't socialize much with them."

Rosie stopped to take another sip of tea and closed her eyes to relish the moment before continuing. "They all said the same thing—no steady boyfriend that they knew of, no noisy parties. Said she was gone a lot, even on weekends. She would stop in the hall and visit with the neighbors, and shared little bits of her life with them, but nothing much on the personal side."

"What about close friends?" Vince asked.

"Her closest friend seems to be her mother. Both her staff and her neighbors say that the mother came around often, particularly in the last several months."

"Is that significant?"

"Her staff didn't think so, only said that she and her mother were close. But I got the impression that Dolores Dunn may have been a helicopter mom, that maybe she was a little too protective. I also got a hint from the staff that the closeness bothered Sandy at times, particularly after it escalated recently."

"You mean before or after Sandy almost died?" Vince asked.

"Yes, it had been happening before, but certainly after."

"The after part sounds reasonable. After all, Sandy did almost die."

"Sure, but . . ." Rosie said with a shrug.

"But what?"

Rosie shook her head. "Nothing really, but I keep wondering why the mother was inserting herself more into Sandy's life these last few months. It seems enough of a change that both the neighbors and her staff mentioned it."

"Okay, that's something to look into. What about other friends?"

"I think her next closest are her staff and a few professional colleagues that she'd periodically have lunch with or meet with at happy hours."

Vince cocked his head to one side. "She did that a lot?"

"No drinking problem, according to all that I spoke with, and her socializing seems limited to short happy hours. About three a week, and they usually include some food. It's a pattern. She'd meet someone, or several people, for a couple of drinks and an appetizer, but they said she almost always went back to her office to work before heading home."

"Sounds like a methodically planned life with no surprises. What about her phone records?"

Rosie gave Vince a knowing grin. "That's my next step. Maybe another pattern will turn up, but only if I can get her permission to go through them. I don't think I have enough to get a search warrant."

She took another sip of tea, looked into the almost empty cup and tossed it into the trash. "What about you? What'd you find about our feisty 76-year old?"

"Well, Gerry Mason is neither so regular nor so well-liked as Sandy. He has few friends, as we would expect, and any socializing seemed to happen when Samuel Jennings was living with him. They'd go out to restaurants regularly or meet friends for drinks, according to Jennings, anyway. My impression was that the friend connections were all from Jennings."

"Did you confirm that?"

Vince gave her a flat look. "Of course. I talked to Gerry's neighbors first and each said about the same thing. He stayed home a lot, was quiet and gave no one grief. No one seemed overly friendly with him, but no one had any unkind words to offer."

"That surprises me."

"Yeah, me too. The worst thing I heard was that he minded his own business, stayed out of everybody else's and mostly kept busy in his studio out back."

Rosie drummed her fingers on the desk, gazed across the room as if wondering what to suggest next. "Did you check out the places he and Jennings used to frequent as a couple?"

Vince waved a hand in the air. "Gerry's abandoned all that socializing. No one at the places Jennings mentioned recognized Gerry's picture—except one, that is. When I went into the Bull Frog, the bartender recognized him and said that Gerry had been there three times over the last couple of months. He even remembered Jennings and Gerry coming in together a couple of years ago. This guy had a great memory."

"So when Gerry was there recently, was he alone?"

He pointed a finger at Rosie. "That's when it gets interesting. Gerry met a guy, the same guy the first two times, and then the same guy and a lady the third and last time."

"So who is this guy? And why was the lady there only once?"

"Don't know that. The bartender said he'd never seen the man before those meetings, or since. He was sure that when Gerry and Jennings came in together, this guy was *not* someone who socialized with them."

"That's one of the few interesting nuggets in either of our investigations." Rosie looked over to the side and tapped her fingers on the desk once more. She glanced across the squad room and noticed that fellow detectives trickled in to start their workday. She turned back to Vince. "What about the lady?"

"The bartender said she wore a big hat that hid most of her face. He didn't get a good look at her, but he remembers what the guy looked like."

"Why don't we ask that bartender to come in and sit with a sketch artist? Let's get a rendering of this guy Gerry met with and run it through facial recognition."

"Good idea. In the meantime, what's your next move?" Vince asked.

"Now that we know Sandy's a defense lawyer, it's time to meet with her again. Defenders connect with some interesting people, people who are capable of lots of things. Maybe I can get her to share something unusual about one or more of her clients."

"Good luck with that," Vince said as he stood and stretched. "That conversation could turn Ms. Congeniality into Ms. No Comment."

Chapter 6

Vince arranged for the bartender from the Bull Frog to sit with one of the department's computer sketch artists. They needed to construct a digital image of the man that Gerry Mason had met with in the bar.

After two hours, the bartender—convinced the sketch on the screen was a perfect rendering of the man—nodded and smiled. "Your guy is good. That sketch looks exactly like him."

Vince's first thought was to ask Mason to identify the person, so he called the hospital to let Mason know to expect a visit. A nurse answered Mason's phone near his bed and said that Mason was in the process of being discharged to home. Based on that, Vince reverted to his original plan to run the sketch through Face Reveal, the department's latest recognition software, and to show the sketch to Mason after he was settled back home if the software didn't come up with a match.

Before any results came up, however, Rosie returned to the office, threw her purse on the desk and fell into a chair with a thud. Grimacing, she looked at Vince. "Tell me you had better luck with the bartender than I did with Sandy Dunn."

A bark of laughter came from Vince. "So the lawyer lawyered-up?"

"You could say that. She said she wants to cooperate and I know she wants to find out the 'what' and 'why' of her near-death event, but she's hiding behind her legal persona."

Vince shook his head. "You won't get anything out of her about her clients. I'll bet she won't even say who may have had a beef with her."

Rosie nodded, gazed around the office, and watched detectives wave in and out of the room. Finally, she said, "I agree. She won't talk about her clients because she feels that no real harm came out of this."

Frowning, Vince asked, "So you're telling me no one threatened her after a verdict went the wrong way? Not one client ever turned hostile toward her?"

"Her exact words were, 'On occasion, I've had disappointed clients, but there were never threats—at least none that I took seriously'. End of quote!"

They were interrupted by a bleep from Vince's computer. He grinned. "Got a facial hit. The guy's sketch matches someone named Joshua Newburg."

"What's he in the system for?" Rosie asked.

"Fraud, specifically art auction fraud."

Her face brightened. "And Gerry Mason's a painter. Could be they're involved in something together and that pissed someone off?"

Vince offered a shrug. "Maybe. The indictment was about eight years ago in New York City. The man pled out, did six months in a minimum-security facility and another three years parole. Nothing new on his sheet since then."

"Do a search. Find out what he's been up to."

"Will do."

Rosie sat straighter in her chair. "Just a thought, while we're talking painters and art fraud. Could the gallery owner where Mason exhibits his work be part of whatever's going on?"

"I guess anything's possible, but—"

"What's his name again?"

"Seth Shapiro . . . The Shapiro Gallery."

"You never told me about your visit with him. He was on your list of interviews."

Vince folded his arms and leaned back. "That's what I was about to tell you. He wasn't available. I called, we talked for a few minutes, but he was late for an appointment. We're supposed to meet at the gallery in the morning."

Rosie tapped her fingers on the desktop. "Okay, you talk to Samuel Jennings again. We need background on Shapiro. In the meantime, I'll dig more into Dunn's life."

Vince leaned forward with a look of curiosity. "What specifically?"

"Phone records."

Vince lowered his brow, squinted an eye. "Good luck getting a court order. Lawyer Sandy won't allow it. She'd cite attorney-client privilege and any judge would back her up."

"I know I'm fishing here, but there has to be a connection between our two victims, and we're going to find it."

Vince nodded his agreement but remained seated. He watched as Rosie reached for her purse and cell phone. She glanced at Vince, stood and walked into the hallway leading to the elevators.

She descended to the lobby, strolled onto the sidewalk and paced for a few minutes—as if gathering enough courage to do something she might regret later. She shook off the feeling and dialed the number.

Frank, her ex-husband, answered on the third ring and they made small talk for a few minutes while Rosie gathered her thoughts, and stalled to gain courage. In the process, she reminded him that they had a long history together and, even though divorced, they were still friends.

She stopped talking for a moment, sighed and blurted out, "I figured with all that phone company power you have, you could get me access to some records—as a favor. I promise I'll make it up to you somehow."

"Do you have a court order?"

She clenched her fists, an edge of frustration in her voice. "Frank, if I did, would I be calling you directly?"

Rosie heard a deep-voiced chuckle before he said, "What do I get out of this?"

When she continued to avoid his questions about how she could repay the favor, her ex laughed.

She looked up at the sky and shook her head. "You're enjoying this a little too much, Frank, and I don't appreciate it. Are you going to help me or not?"

"Okay, I will. But if this ever comes back to haunt me, you won't be able to fix it. I'll be in big trouble."

"No one will ever know. I promise."

"How far back do you want to go?"

"Only this past year." She gave him Sandy Dunn's name and phone number, and waited while he pulled up the records.

After a few moments of silence, he said, "Okay, sending them to your personal email now."

"Thanks, I knew I could count on you."

Rosie hung up, re-entered the building and pressed the elevator button. As she waited, she thought about her relationship with Frank. It had ended badly because of work—her work. He was an executive with the telephone company and supposedly far removed from the dangers of her job. That was the rule—no work ever entered their personal lives. Work always stayed outside the door to their apartment.

Except one night it didn't. A suspect in a case sought revenge because Rosie had accused him of murder, even though she could never get enough evidence to indict him. The idea of a killer entering their apartment and Rosie shooting the suspect to death was something that Frank could not get past. Eventually, their relationship crumbled piece by piece until it was evident that going their separate ways was the only chance they had to remain civil.

The friendship was awkward at first, especially as they both moved into their separate lives, but they kept in touch regularly. Rosie made sure of that. This was the first time, however, that Rosie had actually tested the new relationship.

She walked back into the squad room and eased into her desk chair. Vince's space was empty. She pulled up her personal email and there it was—Sandy Dunn's cell phone records from the last year.

After a methodical examination of calls to same numbers, patterns emerged and Rosie found frequent calls to Sandy's mother, friends and names she assumed to be clients.

Realizing the futility of identifying specific patterns, she looked for familiar phone numbers—specifically any to Gerry Mason, Samuel Jennings, Joshua Newburg or Seth Shapiro. She found a pattern with Seth Shapiro.

Ten calls to him in the last three weeks. Some were for twenty minutes or more. She smiled. The case was beginning to produce leads.

Next, Rosie pulled up courthouse docket records and found that Sandra Dunn was the attorney of record in a recent DUI for Shapiro. The case was eventually dismissed on a technicality, but a civil suit was pending based on an injury to another driver that Shapiro ran into while under the influence.

Rosie grabbed her phone and called Vince. "Where are you?"

"Sitting in my car outside the gallery."

"Why? You said you were going to visit with Jennings today and meet with Shapiro tomorrow."

"I decided not to wait to see Shapiro."

Rosie switched the phone to her other ear. "What changed your mind?"

"My search for Joshua Newburg, that's what. The parole officer I spoke with in New York said the man was a model citizen when he got out, did everything he was supposed to and finally was granted early release from parole after two years. Since then, however, he's fallen off the radar."

"He's disappeared?"

"I found an e-trail on him only until about three months after his parole release. After that, I get nothing. I'm thinking Joshua Newburg became Seth Shapiro."

Rosie squinted. "I assume you did a search on Shapiro to confirm that possibility?"

"All circumstantial, but Shapiro has records that are a bit nebulous also."

"So you can make a connection between the two?"

"Maybe. Shapiro's background indicates he was out of the country, in parts of South America to be exact, until about the time Newburg's trail goes dark."

Rosie smiled knowingly. "The timelines sound too convenient."

"Wait, there's more. I pulled up Shapiro's business records and this guy's gallery is way successful, almost too successful."

"How do you mean?"

"I'm looking at a small building here in an historic but rundown neighborhood. Apparently a lot of business goes through here, but I don't see any activity to indicate that."

Rosie held the phone closer to her face, gestured with her free hand. "Listen to me, Vince. Seth Shapiro, Gerry Mason and Sandy Dunn are all connected."

"How?"

"We know Shapiro's gallery exhibits and sells Mason's paintings. Mason told us that. But I just found out that Dunn is Shapiro's attorney. She represented him in a DUI case and now in a civil suit related to the DUI."

"That's the connection I've been looking for. How'd you find it?" Vince asked.

"Don't worry about that, but stay put. I'm heading your way right now. With this and possibly an alias as Newburg, I don't want you going into that Shapiro interview without backup."

"So now you're my mother?"

"Vince, Shapiro is connected to two people who almost died. I don't know if he's responsible, but you shouldn't be alone when you confront him. Promise me you'll wait for me before going into the gallery."

After a momentary silence, he said, "Okay, but hurry. It's getting hot out here."

Within twenty minutes, Rosie was at the gallery and parked behind Vince's car. She walked over to the driver's side window. The car was empty. She sighed, hit the top of the car with a clenched fist and looked around for any sign of her partner. Seeing no one, she proceeded to the gallery's front door. As she reached for the door, it opened and Vince stood in the doorway.

He seemed startled at first but stood aside and introduced the gallery owner to her. "Mr. Shapiro, this is my partner Detective Rosie Young." To Rosie, Vince added, "Mr. Shapiro and I were discussing a couple of people that we have in common."

Rosie stared into a handsome face that complimented a sturdy but lean frame. It was the same face that showed up on the facial recognition software as Joshua Newburg, only the man in front of her was a little older and sported a fashionable mustache.

She extended a hand as she stared into the man's light green eyes. "Is that so? Was Mr. Shapiro helpful?"

"Somewhat, but he refuses to discuss his legal issues or his attorney."

Seth Shapiro shook Rosie's hand. "What I discuss with my attorney is confidential and my legal issues are . . . well, I'm afraid I'll have to defer to my attorney to answer those questions. I'm sure you understand, Detective."

She nodded and turned to Vince. "And what about Gerry Mason?"

"On that, Mr. Shapiro was more cooperative. Mr. Mason apparently sells a lot of his art through the gallery. He's had several exhibits here."

"Gerry is a valued artist in this community and his work is highly sought after," Shapiro said. He tilted his head in sympathy. "I was sorry to hear about his health issues."

Rosie remained silent, wondered if Vince had confronted Shapiro on his Joshua Newburg alias.

Vince turned to the gallery owner and extended his hand. "Thank you for your time, Mr. Shapiro. I'll be in touch if we need further information."

"I'm sure you will, Detective." Shapiro turned to Rosie. "It was a pleasure to meet you, Detective Young."

As Vince and Rosie walked to their cars, Rosie hit him on the shoulder with a fist. "I thought I told you to wait for me before interviewing that man."

"I would have, but he drove up and gave me a funny look as he walked to the building. I had no choice but to make contact."

She sighed, gave her partner a focused look. "You realize that Seth Shapiro and Joshua Newburg are one and the same."

"I do, and I see that you recognized the resemblance too. But he doesn't understand that we know that fact." Vince pulled out a pen, first wrapping his fist with his handkerchief. "He touched this while we were talking at his desk. He didn't see me take it as I was leaving. Maybe we can pull prints, have hard evidence of who he is before we confront him."

Rosie let out a conspiring laugh. "Good move. So did you learn anything from him?"

"Not much more than what you heard. He referred me back to Dunn for anything that involved her or his legal issues. But when we talked about Mason, he showed me some of Gerry's work. It's pretty good."

"Who brought up Gerry Mason's health issues?"

Vince raised an eyebrow. "He did, said that Samuel Jennings had called him about it and that the exhibit may have to be postponed."

"For not being together anymore, Jennings seems quite involved in Mason's affairs. How did Shapiro take what happened to Mason?" Rosie asked Vince.

"He was concerned, mostly because the exhibit might be delayed, but . . . I don't know how to put it. He seemed troubled about the whole thing, like there was more on the line than only the art exhibit."

"How do you mean?"

"He kept looking away, wouldn't look directly at me when we spoke about Mason or the art exhibit," Vince said.

"Like a 'tell' when someone lies?"

"It was more like he was thinking about a whole lot more than he was saying." Vince gave Rosie a crooked smile. "What I mean is, I got the sense he wasn't exactly lying. His face, however, told me he was hiding the truth about something, something that's not going to happen now that Mason isn't well."

Rosie stopped walking, turned directly to Vince. "You got all that from a facial expression?"

Vince gave her a wide-eyed look. "I tell you, that man seems cool under pressure, and he tactfully evaded all questions about Sandy Dunn, but he started to unravel when we talked about Mason. That's when he played with this pen."

Vince saw that Rosie was waiting for more, like maybe a concluding statement. He said, "I don't know what to do with all this, but something's going on. It's big and it involves Mason."

At that point, Rosie's phone rang. She answered, seemed pleased with what she was hearing and thanked the caller. She disconnected and turned to Vince. "Tox screen is back on Sandy

Dunn. They found something called DMT in her urine sample."

"Dimethyltryptamine? The psychedelic drug people call 'the businessman's trip'?"

Rosie puffed out her lower lip and drew her head back. "Well, look at you, Mr. Chemist. What's dimethyl whatever?"

"It's an hallucinogenic, an illegal recreational drug that's said to give a mind-blowing experience. I read about it recently. People on it lose all sensation, can't even move."

"Really!"

"Yeah, crazy drug, gives a big high, but I don't know much more than that—except that it comes from a vine that grows in the Peruvian rainforest close to the Amazon River."

When Rosie continued looking at him, Vince merely smiled and shrugged. She pulled out her cell phone and dialed a familiar number. "Maybe our favorite ME can give us the scoop on DMT."

She contacted the medical examiners' office, asked to speak to Becky Nolan and was connected to her extension immediately. "Becky, it's Rosie Young. Vince and I have a few questions for you. Can I put you on speaker?"

Without waiting for an answer, Rosie pressed the speaker button on her phone. "What can you tell us about DMT? The lab called and they found that in Sandra Dunn's urine—you know, the girl who died and woke up?"

"I was about to call you. I was just handed the same report and it explains a lot."

Rosie stared at the phone in her hand. "Why, Becky? Talk to me."

"First, dimethyltryptamine is a Schedule I narcotic. That means it's not a legal drug in this country. Some on the street call it 'fantasia' or 'the businessman's special'. It comes from Peru. The indigenous people there used it for centuries to make a brew for healing rituals."

"I see," Rosie said as she glanced toward Vince. "So why use this drug on our victims?"

"DMT gives an extreme rush like heroin, but progresses quickly to loss of all feeling and even the ability to move. People who survive the trip say they were certain they'd died. Interesting that it was found in her urine."

Rosie gave Vince a crisp nod of satisfaction. "Why is that significant, Becky?"

The ME hesitated, as if gathering and organizing her thoughts. "Traces of DMT remain in the bladder for up to five days. A large dose of it can certainly create a comatose state. That would make the user appear dead with virtually no signs of life, but there's a problem with that."

"What kind of problem, Becky?" Rosie held the phone higher and closer to her ear as she narrowed the space between her and Vince.

"It's short-acting. It would not have remained long enough in her system to keep her in a dead-like state overnight like she was."

"But could something else, like maybe another drug, have made that happen?" Vince asked as he pushed the phone away from his eye.

"Hi, Vince. You mean like a drug cocktail? A mixture to sustain the comatose state and yet not kill her?"

Vince nodded, realized that Becky couldn't see the gesture, and said, "Yes. What kind of mix could do that?"

"Let me think. There could be several antidepressant drug possibilities. Monoamine oxidase inhibitors are the first that come to mind, but—oh, of course, it could be baclofen. But maybe that would be overdoing it."

"Why, Becky?" Rosie asked. She shook a clenched hand. "Reason it out for me."

"Baclofen would be a good thing to add because it's widely distributed throughout the body and produces extreme hypothermia, bradycardia, and hyporeflexia. But—"

Rosie rolled her eyes. "In English, Becky."

"Okay, baclofen causes the body temp to lower, slows the heart rate, and produces extreme muscle relaxation. In other words, a person is cool to the touch, has no detectable pulse and no reflex activity as indicators of life. But too much and the person *really* dies, just like with too much DMT."

Vince exchanged a knowing glance with Rosie. He asked, "Could a combo mix of DMT and baclofen make a person seem dead and yet still keep that person alive?"

"It's possible. DMT would free the mind of memory and control, while baclofen would create a death-like comatose state. The mix, however, would have to be specifically-dosed to consider each victim's weight, height, age—that sort of thing."

He smiled at Rosie. "Understood. Becky, do you still have Dunn's fluid samples that you took at the crime scene?"

"Yes, and I'll have the lab test them for baclofen. The drug totally clears in about ten to twenty hours, so that would still be within the window of when I took the samples. They might still be able to detect traces."

"Do you also have fluid samples from Gerald Mason?" Vince asked.

Becky sighed heavily. "No, I never took them because we thought he died of a heart attack since his pacemaker malfunctioned."

Rosie cut in. "But the hospital took samples and they're still being processed."

"Of course!" Becky said. "I'll call the hospital now. I'll order new tests specifically for DMT and baclofen on *his* fluid samples."

"Thanks, Becky, and let us know as soon as you have the results."

Rosie disconnected. She turned to Vince. "I'll go see Sandy Dunn and find out if she took anything recreational or otherwise. I'll also confront her about her connection to Shapiro. You get Shapiro's pen to the lab to confirm that print and go visit with Jennings, see what he says about the *real* relationship between Mason and Shapiro."

Chapter 7

Rosie called Sandy Dunn's cell number, learned that she had returned to work and asked to stop by for a few minutes for more questions. After protesting that she was too busy, Dunn finally agreed and Rosie drove over.

The receptionist at the law office told Rosie to have a seat in the small waiting area, a nicely appointed corner with three cushy chairs, and promised that Dunn would see her momentarily. The moment stretched to a full fifteen minutes, during which Rosie was offered coffee, water, and a variety of out-of-date magazines. As she grew impatient, Dunn walked out of her office to greet the detective.

"Sorry to make you wait. I've been busy trying to catch up on cases. Come in."

Dunn guided the detective down a hall and into an expansive office that stretched across the back of the refurbished house that had been turned into an efficient law office. The attorney pointed to a chair opposite her desk. The detective sat, but Dunn stood behind the desk and rested her hands on the back of her chair.

"Thanks for seeing me on such short notice, Ms. Dunn. I'll be brief. I want to know about your relationship with Seth Shapiro."

Dunn took in a breath and slowly pulled out her chair. She sat behind her desk. "What about him?"

"I know he's a client. That's public record. But he's also connected to a man who experienced the same near death experience as you."

Dunn stiffened, swallowed hard. She tugged on an earlobe and almost pulled out an earring. "There's another one? A person . . . like what happened to me?"

"Yes, and the only common denominator is that you both know Seth Shapiro. What can you tell me about him?"

Dunn glanced around the room, as if looking for an escape route. She lowered the hand that was clutching her earring and clenched her fingers into a fist. "You know I can't talk about clients. That's privileged information."

"Did you know that we believe Seth Shapiro was once known as Joshua Newburg, and that he has a criminal record for art fraud?"

Showing genuine surprise, the attorney took a moment to recover. "I know nothing about that. I'm representing Mr. Shapiro for something completely different."

"Yes, the civil suit for an accident related to a DUI." Rosie pointed to a brochure of Dunn's law practice that was in a holder on the corner of the attorney's desk. "May I take a picture of this brochure? It may help in the investigation."

Dunn crossed her arms. "If it will help . . ."

Rosie pulled out her phone, snapped the picture and sent it to Vince's phone along with the message, "Stop at the Bull Frog before heading to see Jennings. See if the bartender recognizes the woman in the photo."

Dunn stood. "What are you doing?"

"Furthering the case. You were targeted for a reason, and assaulted in a most unusual way. I intend to get to the bottom of it."

Dunn sat, gave a weak nod.

Rosie asked, "Do you know a man named Gerald Mason?"

Looking down and to the left, the attorney said, "Is that the other person who experienced what I did?"

The gesture was not lost on Rosie. She suppressed a smile. "I can't say, but I'd like an answer to my question."

"Why? Is he important to my case?"

"Since you're an attorney, you know that I can't comment on ongoing investigations, even if it involves you." Rosie hesitated a moment, decided to move on to another question. "Do you take any recreational drugs?"

Dunn stood again. "What? Of course not! How dare you even suggest—"

"Counselor, if you keep bobbing up and down like that, you're going to exhaust yourself before I even finish my questions."

The attorney sat, angled her chair sideways and crossed her legs.

"I ask because your lab results came back positive for drugs."

"I don't do drugs, Detective. What did the lab find?"

"DMT, a rather potent recreational substance. It produces an extreme high and, with a large enough dose, it can put a person into a comatose state."

Dunn put a hand to her throat, realized the hand was shaking and lowered it to her lap. "I was drugged? That's why I appeared dead and don't remember anything?"

"It seems so." Rosie pursed her lips, waited for more from Dunn, but got nothing. Dunn remained silent, as if on a witness stand, answering only what was asked.

Rosie decided to move away from the subject of drugs for the time being. That could be discussed later when the full tox screen was available. "Can you tell me if you're representing Mr. Shapiro in any legal matters other than the DUI case?"

"Detective, I've already told you I can't discuss dealings about my clients."

"Even if it involves criminal activity against you personally?"

The attorney stood once again. She swallowed, as if digesting words she could not speak. "This is a waste of time. We're both hiding behind the law. If there's nothing else, I'd like to get back to work now."

Rosie stood, gave the attorney a warm smile. "I hope you realize that I'm on your side. I think you have an idea why someone did this to you. I intend to confirm that and protect you from any additional harm."

"Good day, Detective. I appreciate your concern."

After dropping off the pen at the lab for print analysis, Vince stopped at the Bull Frog to see the bartender. He showed him the picture Rosie sent to his cell phone.

The bartender said, "Yep, that's the woman who met with Mr. Mason and that other guy."

"Did she meet with them more than once?"

"Nope, only that one time."

Vince thanked the bartender and drove to the toy store owned by Samuel Jennings. As he walked into the store, Vince saw Jennings step down from a ladder that stood next to a high shelf in the back corner of the store.

Jennings noticed Vince. "Detective, finally coming back for that police car you liked so much the other day?"

The brief smile from Vince was replaced with a serious look. "I have additional questions for you."

"Okay, let's go back to my office." Jennings descended the ladder, told a clerk where he'd be if needed and escorted the detective to his office. When they settled around his desk, Jennings asked, "What sort of questions? Is Gerry saying stuff about me again?"

"Speaking of Gerry Mason, I was wondering what you know about his relationship with Seth Shapiro, the art gallery owner?"

"How should I know what Gerry's doing now?" Jennings spat out.

"I realize that you're not part of Gerry's life anymore and I understand your bitterness at the break-up, but I'd like you to tell me what you *do* know about him and Shapiro."

Jennings shrugged one shoulder. "It's a simple business deal. Gerry painted pictures, exhibited them at the Shapiro Gallery and Seth sold them. Seth paid Gerry after taking his cut."

"I understand that part, but Gerry and Mr. Shapiro met several times away from the gallery, at the Bull Frog. From what you know about their relationship, does that sound normal to you?"

Jennings scratched his head, gave a brief scowl. "No, not really, but I don't know anything about their dealings after Gerry tossed me out. Gerry and I used to go to the Bull Frog all the time. We'd meet up with friends, but Seth never joined us. And my impression was that Gerry didn't have much of a social life after I was gone."

Vince pulled out his phone. He showed Jennings the picture that Rosie had forwarded to him. "Do you recognize the woman in this photo?"

"She's Seth's attorney and handled a particularly large purchase of Gerry's paintings a few months before Gerry sent me packing. I went with Gerry to the gallery to pick up his check."

"How large a check?"

"Over a hundred grand. Someone purchased almost all of Gerry's paintings that Seth had on hand. Gerry was excited, but at the same time he was freaking out because he knew he had to get back to work to replenish Seth's gallery."

"So Mr. Shapiro wanted more paintings?"

"Yes, he said that Gerry needed to paint faster because his paintings were getting so popular and he needed to take advantage of that."

Vince turned his head to one side and smiled. "A nice arrangement for them. It's not often that a relatively unknown artist gets noticed so well."

"Certainly both would benefit from Gerry having more paintings available for sale at the gallery, and they were both thrilled about it. But . . ."

"But what, Mr. Jennings?"

"Well, certainly I expected that Seth would want more of what he'd just sold, but he really pressured Gerry to produce—as if he needed quantity over quality."

Vince shifted in his chair and furrowed a brow. "What did Gerry say about that?"

"He got very focused on his work, put himself under tremendous pressure to paint. That turned him into a grumpy old man. He complained about all the little things that irritated him, especially the stuff he thought I did wrong."

Jennings gazed at the walls of his office, eventually looked down at his desk and folded his hands over a rounded belly. "We fought often about the time he spent painting, and that evolved into rants about the weight I'd gained over the years. Finally, Gerry's art career won out and I got the boot."

Vince scratched his head, pondered how to ask his next question. "Do you know anything about Seth Shapiro's background, about how he became an art dealer?"

"It never occurred to me to ask. That's Gerry's business, not mine."

"I guess I mean what qualified him to sell art? And who buys what he exhibits? I was over at his gallery recently. There was no customer traffic while I was there."

Jennings shrugged that same shoulder. "I never thought about it much, at least until that big check came in for Gerry. I don't know how an art dealer works his trade, but I suspect it's nothing like my business here. I rely on foot traffic into the store for sales. My impression is that an art dealer makes connections between buyers and artists, and sometimes that's not even in person."

"Is Gerry that good? Is his work that popular?"

Jennings scrunched up his mouth. "It's not my taste, but who knows? I've definitely seen worse."

"One last question: Have you heard the name Joshua Newburg?"

"Not that I recall. Why?"

"Just a name that came up in Gerry's case." Vince stood. "I appreciate the time. I'll be in touch if we need anything else."

Vince turned and started to walk out of the office, but he stopped and twisted around to ask one more question. "I almost forgot. I understand that you called Mr. Shapiro to let him know about Gerry's pacemaker malfunction. That was kind of you, but why care about Gerry's work with the gallery?"

Samuel Jennings frowned and remained speechless for a moment. Finally, he smiled. "Just because I think Gerry's an ass doesn't mean that I wish him any misfortune. I wanted the gallery to know that Gerry might not make his deadline for the next showing. I was hoping Seth could reschedule it for a later date. I'd hate for Gerry to lose out on the great arrangement he made with Seth."

Chapter 8

While sitting in his car outside the toy store, Vince called Rosie. He confirmed that the bartender recognized Sandy Dunn's picture as the woman who met with Mason and Shapiro the last time they were in the bar. He also confirmed that Jennings identified Dunn as Shapiro's lawyer in his art dealings.

"That's what I thought, but Dunn wouldn't confirm it," Rosie said.

"As Shapiro's attorney, confidentiality would be normal practice."

"It would be normal to decline any comment about Shapiro's legal dealings, but she can say that she's his lawyer. Why hide that simple fact?"

"Maybe she suspects something isn't right with Shapiro's business?"

"Could be, Vince, or maybe she's afraid to say anything. Could be that Shapiro threatened her, or even did this to her to keep her silent about something."

"In that case, he should have killed her. Why almost dead and not really dead? I think there's more to this than we're seeing," Vince said.

"Agreed. Look, it's been a long day and we've learned a lot. Let's pick it up again in the morning, put a fresh set of eyes on the case after a good night's sleep. I'm going to stop by the hospital on my way home to check on Mason. I'll get his impression of Shapiro. Maybe he'll have something new to add to what we already know."

"You do that, Rosie. I've got a date with a beer, a bag of salted nuts and a soft bed."

Rosie drove to San Antonio General Hospital and took the elevator to the surgical floor. She stopped at the nurses' station, got permission to visit for a few minutes and headed to Mason's room. She knocked gently on the door before entering.

"What is it now? These interruptions are going to give me a heart attack!"

Sticking her head into the room, Rosie said, "Thought you could use some company. Can I come in for a few minutes?"

Mason leaned back into the two pillows propping him up and waved her in. "Oh, it's you. Sure . . . I thought it was that pesky nurse. She's always coming in to take my blood pressure, temperature or whatever. Enough to make my pressure go through the roof."

"Now calm down. Stressing out over good medical care isn't healthy."

He pointed a finger at her and scowled. "Young lady, you find my almost-killer and that'll make me stop stressing."

"We're working on it. Gerry, can I ask you some questions?"

He rolled his eyes and chuckled. "If I said no, I'm sure you'd ask anyway."

Rosie shrugged and gave him a sly grin. "It looks like the more we dig into your case the more we need to know. I'm sorry to bother you but I need information only you can provide."

He sat straighter in the bed and frowned. "What are you talking about—what information?"

"You do a lot of business with the Shapiro Gallery. For starters, how well do you know Seth Shapiro? I'd like to learn more about his background in art dealing, and why you chose his gallery to sell your paintings."

He folded his arms over his chest. "Seth has been a good friend. He's helped my career take off. I can never thank him enough."

"So he was a friend before he became your art dealer?"

He unfolded his arms and looked at her like she had grown a second nose. "That's not what I said. He's my friend *because* his gallery pays me well for my paintings. I paint. He sells them. He pays me—after his generous commission, I might add. He makes it simple for me to do what I love best—paint!"

"So how did you meet him? How did he learn about your work?"

"From Tom, Thomas Muñoz."

"Who's that, a friend of yours?"

"Yes . . . well, a friend of mine as well as Sam's."

"Samuel Jennings?"

"Yes, Sam actually knew Tom from before we were together. Sam introduced us and we'd meet at a bar in the evening for drinks, happy hours and that sort of thing. When Tom realized I was a painter, he wanted to see my work. I guess he liked my paintings because he talked to Seth Shapiro about me. Seth displayed a couple of pieces. They sold, so Seth took on a few more."

"What does Thomas Muñoz do for a living?"

"He restores art, takes old paintings that have been damaged in some way and brings them back to life. Although I haven't seen his work, he told me that Seth was a client."

Rosie smiled and nodded. "Thanks, Gerry. I should let you get some rest now."

Mason chuckled. "Sure . . . pump me for information and toss me aside. Find out who did this to me, Detective, and I'll rest . . . not before."

Chapter 9

Rosie went home feeling that the case was producing tidbits of new information. She knew that was often how cases got solved—in a slow, steady, painstaking process. Find a crumb of evidence here, a new lead there. Add in a bit of persistence and suddenly a pattern would evolve and the bigger picture would come into focus.

She needed the final tox screen results on both Dunn and Mason, but that would take a few more days. She got a good night's sleep and arrived at the station rested and ready to go over the case details with her partner.

Vince was already at his desk. He took the last bite of an egg and sausage sandwich, wiped greasy hands on a napkin and looked up at her. "Don't get too comfortable. We have a body at the morgue."

"I suspect there's more than one there. What makes this one so important?" Rosie questioned with a deadpan look.

Vince tilted his head, gave her an exasperated look. "Because we knew the corpse. It's Samuel Jennings. He was murdered last night."

"*What?* Why didn't someone call us?"

"Because we weren't on rotation last night and the team on call didn't connect the dots to our cases until this morning. Thanks to our captain, the case is now ours."

Rosie blew out a big breath and her eyes widened at the news. Vince said, "Yeah, crazy, isn't it? We should get going. Becky Nolan's the ME on the case. She's waiting for us at the morgue."

Vince stood, threw the remains of his breakfast into the trash and trotted to the elevator. Rosie switched her purse to the other shoulder, rushed to catch up with him and was able to squeeze into the elevator just before the doors closed on her.

They drove in silence for a few minutes until Rosie said, "Mason told me something last night about Jennings that disturbed me. I was waiting until this morning to brief you, but I think Jennings might be behind all this."

"Not any longer. He's now a bigger piece of an even bigger puzzle."

Rosie told Vince about stopping at the hospital to see Mason, said Mason told her how he met Shapiro and that she did an Internet search on Thomas Muñoz after getting home. "I learned that Muñoz was indicted for art forgery and spent several years in jail."

"And Seth Shapiro, aka Joshua Newburg, was in jail for art fraud. Coincidence?" Vince asked.

Rosie gazed through the car's windshield. She focused on the morning traffic for a few moments, watched as a couple of drivers sped through a yellow traffic light. Finally, she said, "Probably not. Granted, those were separate cases, separate trials, separate crimes. But Shapiro and Muñoz were in the same prison at the same time. It had to be where they met."

Vince tapped the steering wheel and cut his eyes toward Rosie. "So when Muñoz got out, he somehow made friends with Jennings and then with Mason . . . and that's how Mason hooked up with Shapiro?"

"Yes, I think, to all of that," Rosie said as she scrunched up her forehead. "What I don't understand, though, is why Dunn and Mason were almost killed. It must have been to scare them into silence, but why? And why is Jennings now dead?" She turned to her partner. "He really is dead, isn't he?"

"We'll find out soon enough."

They arrived at the morgue. Vince parked while Rosie waited in the lobby and they went down the hall together to Becky's office. The ME was sitting with her head held between her hands, elbows resting on the desk. When she saw the detectives, her face brightened.

"Good, you're here. When I found out that the Jennings murder and your cases were connected, I wasn't sure if I should put a guard on the body or what."

"So is Jennings dead or not?" Rosie asked.

Becky wrinkled her nose. "I think so, but these days one really can't be sure. His throat was slashed. He bled out."

Vince chuckled. "Well, I guess that makes him *really* dead."

Becky waved a hand in the air. "Of course, but I had another ME check over the body before I did the autopsy just to be sure. Sorry, but the other detectives viewed the autopsy before we realized this one was going to be your case also. If I'd had any idea . . ."

"No worries, Becky, we've got it now. It was definitely a murder, not suicide?" Vince asked.

"Oh, it was definitely murder. The slash went from one ear to the other. No way someone could have done that to himself and completed the swipe. His head was almost cut clean off. This was up close and personal."

"Any prints on the victim, or a weapon?" Rosie asked.

Vince held up a finger to interject a thought, but Becky chimed in. "Oh, you don't know? The victim had hidden security cameras all around his house, inside and out. The other detective team said the cameras recorded it all."

Turning to Rosie, Vince gave her a shy grin. "That's what I was going to tell you. The other team is turning everything over to us. The footage is being sent over as we speak. The crime lab processed the video and got a good visual of the murderer. I was so interested on the way over to hear about your update and theory about Muñoz that I didn't have a chance to tell you."

Rosie drew back, gave Vince a long look and rested a hand on each hip. "You could have interrupted me."

She turned to Becky. "Let's see the body for the record and we'll want a copy of the autopsy."

"Of course."

They followed Becky to the autopsy room and went to the center table. Becky pulled back the sheet and displayed the victim's throat. "No other wounds, no defensive cuts on the arms or hands. The victim was in his bed when I arrived at the home. He bled out there."

"Who discovered the body?"

"A college-aged niece who was in town for a few days to stay with her uncle before heading back to school. The girl was out with friends, but said that Jennings insisted that she let him know when she came home. After knocking on his bedroom door and getting no response, she peeked in and found him dead."

"Where's the girl now?" Rosie asked Becky.

"She was pretty shaken up and wanted to leave the uncle's house as soon as possible. I calmed her down before some officers took her statement. After that, they drove her to a friend's house."

"It's all in the report," Vince said with a wave of his hand.

Rosie turned to Vince, pressed her lips together and shook her head. "So I guess we'd better head back to the office to check out the videos then. If that footage can identify who did this, we'll close this case and maybe find out how it fits in with the Dunn and Mason cases."

When the detectives returned to the station, they reviewed the evidence report that was turned over to them. There were no surprises or complications.

The victim was brutally murdered in his own bed while carefully hidden video equipment recorded it all, even the anguished scene of the victim's niece discovering the body.

Vince pulled a couple of full-face snapshots of the murderer from the video and began a facial recognition search before delving into the rest of the report.

As he thumbed through the report, he said, "The crime scene techs state that they found no trace evidence on the victim or in the near vicinity of the body, and no unidentifiable prints were found at the scene."

"That alone is suspicious. Let's go interview the niece. Maybe she'll remember something she forgot earlier," Rosie said.

The detectives were about to go interview the niece when Face Reveal got a hit. The face came back as Thomas Muñoz.

"Forget the niece. Let's find Muñoz," Rosie said with a smile.

They contacted Muñoz's parole officer, confirmed a last known address and went there. All was quiet in a subdued neighborhood on the near north side of downtown. They strolled up the sidewalk to the house, checking for movement in the windows as they did, but found none. Vince moved to the back of the house while Rosie drew her weapon and inspected the front door. It was locked. As planned, one minute later each detective kicked in a door. They entered shouting, "Police, hands up."

Silence was the only response. They began a methodical search of each room and found Muñoz sprawled on the kitchen floor in a pool of blood.

"I'll call EMS," Vince shouted as he pulled out his phone.

Rosie checked for a pulse. The wrist was cool to the touch. "Never mind. He's dead. Shot in the head at close range, front to back."

"The rear door was locked, no sign of forced entry," Vince said.

Rosie nodded. "Front door also. Muñoz most likely knew his killer and let that person in. The killer probably relocked the door on the way out."

"The back door has a simple push button lock on it."

"Front door too." Rosie observed the victim without touching anything. "Looks like a small caliber wound, possibly from a .22—maybe a concealed pistol Muñoz didn't see until it was too late. Get the crime scene techs here pronto."

Chapter 10

As with the Jennings case, the Muñoz crime scene produced no murder weapon, but the detectives did find vials of drugs and other paraphernalia at Muñoz's house. These were sent to the lab for analysis. They also found files on hypnosis and subliminal suggestions. They had the victim's car towed to police impound and lab techs pulled the car's GPS history.

Two specific trips from the GPS logs were significant. One was from the city morgue to Dunn's apartment and the other to Mason's house from the funeral home where his body was being prepped for burial.

The following day, Rosie and Vince asked Becky Nolan to stop by for an evidence review of the connected cases. The detectives and the medical examiner stood in front of an evidence board near the detectives' desks. The white board, four by eight feet long and on a stand, had bits of written evidence and pictures taped on it in chronological order. Vince added the words "Baclofen found in blood trace" next to Sandy Dunn's picture.

Rosie turned to Becky. "We need your help to sort out and explain the drugs used here. The lab report states that the vials recovered from Muñoz's home contained DMT, baclofen and midazolam."

Becky studied the board and nodded. She turned to the detectives. "The right amounts of DMT and baclofen combined could produce a comatose state that would make the person appear dead, with no detectable reflexes for up to 12 hours, maybe longer. Shallow breathing and a slowed heart rate cools the body sufficiently to make the person appear dead. There'd be enough blood flow in the veins, however, to prevent clotting so the person wouldn't actually die of an embolism. There'd be an adequate KVO rate."

"What's KVO?" Rosie asked.

"It means 'keep vein open'—that's a slow blood flow rate, but it's fast enough to keep clots from forming in the veins."

"Ingenious," Vince said. "And that might have been enough to slow Mason's heart rate to almost nothing so that his pacemaker malfunctioned, even a piezoelectric nanoparticle one like he had in him."

Becky nodded. "That's a reasonable conclusion, and a good reason why the doctors wanted to replace it with a newer model."

He went to his desk and picked up several photos. He walked to the board and put up pictures of a dart gun, dart syringes and drug vials next to Muñoz's picture. "Becky, what about the midazolam?"

"It's used in short duration surgeries to knock a person out. It puts them into a brief twilight sleep. It's called conscious sedation, but they don't remember a thing."

"So this is what Muñoz used to initially sedate Dunn and Mason?"

"I believe so. Midazolam is a high affinity benzodiazepine—"

"In English, Becky," Rosie said.

Becky sighed, drew in a deep breath and let it trickle out while she gathered her thoughts. "The drug is marketed as Versed and it works quickly. A 2mg dose is 1cc of liquid—the same amount that fits into those dart syringes. It would put someone into a sedated state immediately and they wouldn't remember what happened to them after that. But at the same time, they'd be receptive to hypnotic suggestions."

Vince walked back to his desk and picked up the evidence bag that contained the folders he took from Muñoz's house. "All this info on hypnotic techniques and subliminal suggestions—could someone actually be programmed to wake up and go back home at a certain time after being drugged first with midazolam and then with a DMT-baclofen cocktail?"

"I'm no expert on hypnosis, but that's what I understand. The way I see it, Muñoz broke the windows to gain access and shot a dart filled with midazolam through the windows to put Dunn and Mason into a conscious sedative state before they realized what was happening." Her hands moved across the board as she justified her theory. "Next, he entered and performed hypnosis to get them to do what he wanted them to when they woke up. Finally, he administered the DMT-baclofen drug mix to put them into a comatose state that essentially mimicked death."

"But how could he be so sure they'd wake up on schedule and come back home? And why do that in the first place?" Vince asked.

Becky studied the board closely and scanned the evidence for a few moments before stepping back. "There'd have to be some sort of trigger to wake them up—like a word, a phrase or maybe some music—before they'd act on a subliminal hypnotic suggestion."

Rosie shook her head like she didn't comprehend what was being said. "But they were asleep, essentially dead, Becky. And no one was around when they woke up."

"True, so the only other way—a better way actually since they were comatose—would be to use some sort of electrical stimulus, something that would shock them out of a drugged sleep."

"But, Becky, both were alone. Camera surveillance at the morgue as well as at the funeral home confirms that. The footage in both cases shows that they simply woke up, got dressed and walked out," Rosie said.

The ME nodded and focused on the pictures of Dunn and Mason attached to the board. She frowned as she spoke. "There's really nothing simple about this. Maybe there's . . . yes, that has to be it. There has to be an implanted chip in both of them and that chip produced the signal to wake them up." She turned to the detectives with a look of satisfaction.

Vince gave Becky a perplexed look in return. "Wouldn't you have found a chip when you examined them at the morgue?"

"That would be true if I had done an autopsy on *either* of them. Remember, I got backed up and didn't get a chance to schedule the one on Dunn until *the next day*—and by then she was gone. And Mason got signed out to the funeral home *without* an autopsy."

Vince glanced at Rosie. He saw her nod and smile. He turned back to Becky. "So we have to get both examined to find those chips. What do we do, X-rays?"

"Yes, a full body X-ray would detect them. Send both victims to San Antonio General Hospital. They have a machine that can do that. And while we're there, let's schedule for an expert hypnotist to interview them."

"Why? What will that do?" Rosie asked.

"If they were hypnotized to respond to a chip to make them wake up, get dressed and go back home, we may be able to find that out through additional hypnosis to recover those lost memories. The subconscious mind holds all of your memories, beliefs and behaviors. They're never really lost. We might be able to recover the memories we need."

"Okay, Becky, you make the arrangements with the hospital. Dunn and Mason both want answers, so I'm sure Vince and I can have them there whenever you set it up."

"Give me a couple of days to find an expert hypnotist and to schedule the body scans. By then, I should also have the rest of the tox screen results on Dunn and the ones for Mason." Becky scanned the entire evidence board one more time. She nodded and smiled. "I think we're finally getting somewhere. The science is starting to make sense."

After the ME left, Rosie and Vince returned to the evidence board. Each studied it in silence for a few more moments, absorbing as much detail as they could.

Finally, Rosie turned to Vince. "What Becky suggested could solve part of the case—how Muñoz got to Dunn and Mason, and how they got through a night of being mostly dead but woke up and went home the next morning. What we still don't know, though, is *why* he did it."

Vince pointed to the picture of Seth Shapiro on the board and tapped it. "This man is the common denominator. He's Dunn's client. He worked with Mason and probably became friends with Muñoz in prison. From his print on that pen, we've confirmed that Shapiro is really Joshua Newburg.

"I suspect that Shapiro wanted to control Dunn and Mason for some unknown reason. Maybe he had Muñoz plant a hypnotic suggestion to have them forget something important, something that Shapiro didn't want them remembering at all."

Rosie turned her gaze to the dusty windows at the far end of the squad room. She seemed to look past them, as if deep in thought, then glanced back at Vince. "Sounds plausible. But why did Muñoz murder Jennings? That crime has to be connected to Shapiro, but how?"

"Let's split up. We'll do separate research like before. You dig into Shapiro's past and I'll dig into

Muñoz's. Something's bound to pop up that ties back to Jennings, Dunn and Mason."

Rosie nodded. "That's a good plan. We'll meet up in the morning to compare notes."

Chapter 11

The man entered Seth Shapiro's office without knocking. Shapiro looked up from his computer as the rough-looking guy slumped into a chair facing the desk and dangled one leg over the chair arm. Shapiro focused on the man's dusty boots and gave him a disapproving glance. With an unconcerned look, the man swung his leg down and leaned his elbows on jean-clad knees. Taunt arm muscles twitched under the sleeves of his tight tee shirt, his tattoos moving in unison with the ripple of flesh.

Most people knew the man only as Angel—no last name, no history—but Shapiro had met him in prison and they'd worked together ever since.

Angel nodded at Shapiro, a gesture that included a sneer and reeked of crudeness. The scar across his chin gave off a slight sheen. "You want to see me?"

"I have another shipment for you to deliver. A private jet will arrive tonight at Stinson Field, eight o'clock sharp. You'll be there to hand over the paintings, twelve in all. Don't be late. The plane will only be on the ground for a few minutes before continuing on its journey."

"Is everything ready? I'll load 'em up now."

"They're in the process of being crated as we speak. You can wait out front if you wish." Shapiro picked up a pen to sign a check and a document that he had printed out earlier.

Angel looked at his watch, pushed some wayward strands of greasy hair out of his face and stood. "I'll catch some dinner. Be back in an hour."

The man turned to leave, but Shapiro blurted out, "Are you sure you've covered all our tracks? They'll remember nothing?"

The man turned slowly and lifted one side of his mouth into a grin. "You mean Dunn and Mason? Relax, will ya? I told you, Muñoz is good—or was good." Angel chuckled. "They'll never remember a thing. Before he knocked 'em out for the night, I asked Muñoz to plant a hypnotic suggestion—one of his special threats. He always liked to threaten his victims—looked forward to seeing the look of fear on their faces."

Shapiro let out a sigh and tossed the pen onto his desk. "He was a sick man! It was a better plan than murder, but was it enough? I wanted Sandy and Gerry to survive but not complicate things, and to never find out the truth. Sandy's been a great lawyer, a one in a million jewel. And Gerry cooperates. He paints like a robot. It's just . . ."

"Just what? That they overheard a conversation and you needed that fixed? I fixed it!" Angel said. He jutted out his chin and pushed back hair that had fallen over one eye. "You said keep 'em alive but scare the hell out of 'em—and that's exactly what I did. Muñoz said he told both that if they ever remembered and said anything about the weird painting shipments going out of the country, they'd not be *almost* dead but *really* dead the next time.

He said a suggestion like that under hypnosis would . . . well, he's sure they got the message loud and clear."

"But you didn't do it yourself. You got Muñoz to do your dirty work, and then had him kill Jennings."

Angel threw up his hands. "Are you stupid or somethin', man? Jennings had to go. The police were snooping around him like flies on shit. He'd have talked his way to jail, with us right there with him."

"I get it, Angel, but did you have to kill Muñoz so soon after Jennings?"

"Look, with him and Jennings out of the way, there's no one left to rat us out. End of story!"

Shapiro nodded and told Angel to grab some dinner, that the paintings would be ready when he returned. After he left, Shapiro closed the lid on his laptop and stretched to relieve the tension in his back. It was time for his appointment with Gerry Mason. He folded the document he signed earlier and put a check into the folds of the document. He stuffed them into his suit coat before putting it on and walking to his car. He drove to Mason's bungalow.

Three knocks later Shapiro watched as Mason approached the ornate glass door. Mason opened it and welcomed a smiling Shapiro into his home.

"So good of you to come over with the check. I'd go to your office, but I'm still feeling at bit off from my pacemaker surgery."

"No problem, Gerry. Happy to stop by."

Mason led the way into his living room and offered a comfortable chair to Shapiro. Mason walked around the coffee table with an unsteady gait and sat on the couch facing him. "So you've sold the last of my paintings?"

"The last six are being delivered this evening. I have your payment and a detailed accounting breakdown for your records." Shapiro's hand dipped into his suit coat pocket. He pulled out the check and document. He reached across the table and handed them to Mason. "This brings up the subject of further business. I know you've had a medical setback, but the next showing of your work is in two weeks."

Mason scanned the accounting record and check. "You sold them all to one buyer?"

"A collector—he may resell them. Who knows? It gets complicated sometimes with expensive art."

"That's why I cherish you so much, Seth. I paint and you take care of the details."

"The details are that I'll need six more paintings in two weeks. Tell me that's possible."

Mason shrugged, a slight frown appeared on his face. "It's doable. I finished three before my . . . my health crisis. Another two are almost done. Finishing those and one more in a couple of weeks won't be a problem."

"Good to hear, and I'm glad you're still comfortable with the arrangement. The schedule is extremely important since I feature your work so often at gallery parties."

"No, I'm fine with the painting schedule. It seemed tight at one time, but I have a rhythm going now. So . . . no problem."

Shapiro smiled. He stood to leave. "Well, Gerry, I'll let you get back to your work. I'll be in touch soon."

Gerry looked down at the check again. "Thank you."

At precisely eight o'clock, Angel drove up to the private hangar at Stinson Municipal Airport, a short six-mile journey south of San Antonio's downtown business district. He killed the headlights on the large Cadillac SUV, lowered the driver's side window and waited. Shortly, he heard the high-pitched whine of a jet approaching, the engines winding down as the sleek plane descended toward the runway.

The Gulfstream V landed with a momentary squeal as idle tires connected with concrete. The jet slowed and taxied to the hangar. The passenger door opened and light from the plane's interior cascaded to the tarmac. A set of stairs unfolded to the ground and a floodlight switched on to illuminate the stairs.

A man, likely the pilot given the uniform he wore, descended—his silhouette backlit, his face in shadow. The uniformed man stood on the bottom step and folded his arms.

That was Angel's signal to move. He started the engine, put the SUV in gear and drove the short distance to the plane. He got out, walked around to the back, and opened the large rear door. He gazed at the twelve, crated paintings stacked three high in four piles. The back seats, when folded down, created a large cargo area.

The 16 x 24 inch paintings were crated in thin, rectangular wooden boxes about twice the thickness of the framed paintings. The four corners of each were reinforced with triangular wooden blocks, each block secured with a wing nut.

Angel lifted a crate in each arm, walked to the plane's steps and handed them to the pilot, who ascended the stairs and transferred the crates to faceless hands. The same ritual repeated six more times.

After the last hand-off, the pilot remained at the top of the stairs. He waved to Angel and pressed a button. The floodlight switched off as the stairs folded into the side of the plane. With the stairs tucked away, the door closed. Soon the jet's engines started and the plane moved away from the hangar with its engines revving up.

Angel returned to the SUV and sat. He stared through the windshield and watched as the jet taxied to the end of the runway. The jet's engines roared as it rolled down the runway, slowly at first, and picked up speed until it soared into the darkened sky. Angel started the SUV, put it in gear and drove off the airport property into the night.

Chapter 12

The next morning, Rosie arrived at the office before dawn. Surprised that Vince was already at his desk and working at his computer, she said, "Beat me here again? If I didn't know better, I'd say you were competing for my job!"

When he looked up, she noticed dark circles under his eyes and the same wrinkled shirt he had worn the previous day. She tilted her head and frowned. "You didn't go home last night."

Vince shrugged, rubbed tired eyes and pointed to his computer screen. "Get a cup of coffee and settle in. I have interesting news for you."

Rosie plopped down into her chair. She pulled a travel mug from her oversized bag. "Way ahead of you. Spit it out."

"Okay, so yesterday we were obsessing about how Shapiro's connected to Muñoz, Mason and Dunn—but we weren't getting anywhere. Since Shapiro seemed to be the common denominator, I examined his life year by year starting with his indictments for art fraud."

"You found something useful?"

"I uncovered possible new connections. We know Seth Shapiro and Thomas Muñoz were in prison together—both because of separate art fraud convictions. According to the warden I spoke with last night, they also became friends with other prisoners while behind bars."

She put the folder down and sat straighter in her chair. "Why did *that* specifically get the warden's attention? Prisoners bond with each other all the time behind bars."

After tucking in his wrinkled shirt, Vince said, "Because two other inmates were often on kitchen duty at the same time as Shapiro and Muñoz—all model prisoners given the privilege of helping prepare those fine prison meals. The warden remembered because the kitchen guard asked for all four to be assigned there since they worked well together."

"Who are the other two and where are they now?"

Vince scratched his head and smiled. "Both are out of prison at present. One is named Alex Rojas. I'm tracing his whereabouts now—so far the trail is a bit complicated and I'll need more time to locate him. The other is Angel Moreno. He was easier to find and that trail got interesting real fast."

"Oh? Why's that?" Rosie asked.

Vince pulled a computer-generated photo from a folder, stood and walked to the evidence board still positioned near their desks. He stuck the picture with a bit of tape between the ones of Shapiro and Muñoz already taped to the board. Next he picked up a marking pen and wrote a black plus sign between the new picture and each of the other two. He tapped the middle picture with his knuckle.

"I think Angel Moreno is the missing puzzle piece in our cases. He was in prison for beating a guy to death. The charge was first degree murder, but a 'heat of passion' defense with the circumstances being a drunken brawl in a bar earned him only a light sentence." Vince scrunched up one side of his mouth and lifted an eyebrow.

Rosie's gaze moved from Vince to Moreno's picture and back. "Your face tells me there's more."

"Seems Angel's been around death before. There was a previous charge of murder, but it was dropped and ruled self-defense. Then there was a vehicular manslaughter charge a couple of years before that, but he got off with some community service since they couldn't prove lethal intent."

"Didn't I hear someone in our gang unit mention that the Mexican Mafia had an assassin they called the 'Angel of Death'? I think they said the assassin's been in the wind for a while. You think this is the guy?" Rosie asked.

"That's the first thing I thought too, but I can't establish a link between him and any Mafia activity. I'll will tell you that his life has more holes in it than a piece of Swiss cheese."

Rosie thought about Vince's statement, tried to connect the invisible dots. Finally, she shook her head, took a step back and studied the board again, but gave Vince a perplexed look. "Gaps in a person's history can be explained by connections to gangs, particularly if he did a good job of keeping the spotlight off that part of his life, but we'll need more to connect him to our cases."

Vince smiled. "I think I've got it. That's what I've been leading up to."

Rosie nodded and smirked. "Typical—stringing me along. You've been setting me up just now so you can announce the big break you discovered in these cases, haven't you?"

"I have. I discovered that Angel Moreno is back in San Antonio and he's on Shapiro's payroll."

"He works for Shapiro and you didn't tell me that up front?" Rosie blurted out.

Vince laughed. "You had to hear his background first. It only makes sense that he's involved if he has a history around death *and* he's currently associated with the gallery. Although I don't see any evidence of a job description so far, I did find that Angel gets large bonuses from the gallery on a regular basis."

Chapter 13

Sandy Dunn drove to the Shapiro Gallery, parked in the side lot and walked to the front door. She took a deep breath, squared her shoulders and stepped inside. When her eyes adjusted from bright sunlight to the dim gallery lighting, she continued her journey to Shapiro's office.

Halfway to the elevator, a female employee with a broad smile approached. Sandy held up a hand and gestured to the second floor. "I'm here to see Mr. Shapiro."

The employee nodded and moved aside so Sandy could continue to the elevators. When the doors opened, a bulky guy stood near the back of the elevator. His build was that of a professional wrestler. Sandy knew him as Shapiro's personal . . . she couldn't find the words in her mind to describe his exact job title. His name was Angel, but his demeanor was definitely not angelic. He was polite, yet his manner was demanding, gruff and always with a determined look pasted on his face.

What seemed odd to Sandy was that he instantly appeared every time she met with Shapiro and the man remained nearby. He was introduced once as Shapiro's assistant, but there was already someone who handled most of Shapiro's paperwork and communications.

Angel's presence in the elevator unnerved her. His arm and neck tattoos evidenced a prison experience. A quick glance at his neck showed a typical cobweb tat that indicated the passage of time behind bars and the spider in the center told of past drug addiction. The arm sleeve of tats was a mix of chains, locks, hourglasses and an interesting large eye looking out from behind brass bars. As a defense attorney, Sandy had seen her share of prison art and knew each detail had a particular meaning.

He grinned, bowed and gestured with his hands for Sandy to enter the small space. As Angel tilted his head forward, greasy strands of hair cascaded to his forehead. After a moment's hesitation, she complied and they rode up to the second floor without any verbal exchange.

The elevator stopped at the upper level and the doors slowly opened. She squeezed out before the door had fully slid out of her way and glanced back before continuing down a short hall to Shapiro's office. A female receptionist in an outer office area announced Sandy's arrival. Angel appeared by her side, silently and without warning, and ushered her into his boss's office.

Shapiro stood behind his desk. He smiled pleasantly when Sandy walked in. Angel's muscular forearm invited her to sit. She declined.

"I came as soon as I heard," she said. "You have a new artist you'll be working with?"

"A new talent I've recently discovered. I'll need a similar artist contract, like the one we used for Gerry Mason, but with more explicit terms."

"What specifically do you want changed?"

"I'll need a new painting every week and I'd like you to add a rather severe clause for failure to deliver."

An unsettled feeling formed deep within her, a reaction that she could not explain nor resist. Goose pumps exploded along her arms and back. "Is Mr. Mason not able to provide further services?"

Shapiro glanced briefly at Angel before turning back to her with a patient grin. "Gerry will continue to paint, but he's had a medical setback and is behind in his work. It's time to groom another up-and-coming artist."

Sandy swallowed hard. "A medical setback? Is he going to be okay?"

Shapiro realized everyone was still standing and gestured to chairs in front of his desk. "Please, take a seat and don't concern yourself with him. We have a new contract to work on. Here's what I want you to do."

Chapter 14

As Rosie contemplated the role Angel Moreno may have played in the death of Jennings and Muñoz, and more importantly how she and Vince could prove his involvement, her cell phone rang. She looked around the squad room for a second, realized that it was her phone ringing and answered the call from the medical examiner.

"Hi, Becky, you have those lab results for me?"

"You're such a mind reader, Rosie. Of course I do, and they're what I expected, *plus* a lot more."

"You sound thrilled. You've found something significant?" Rosie looked across her desk toward Vince, who was sitting at his. He gave Rosie a frown and lifted his arms and shoulders as if the gesture was a silent question.

Rosie put her hand over the phone and whispered, "ME calling with more test results." Vince nodded with a satisfied grin. Rosie returned her focus to the phone call. "So, Becky, tell me what's got you so excited."

"I think I've worked out the details on how Sandra Dunn and Gerald Mason *sort* of died, came back to life, got themselves home, but remembered nothing about any of it."

"Great. Start from the beginning," Rosie said.

"Okay, we know it all started with a dart. More specifically, it was a dart syringe that delivered the dose of Versed and scopolamine which knocked the victims out—well, maybe not knocked them out physically as in on the floor, but . . ."

Rosie rolled her eyes, stared across the squad room and rubbed fingers across her forehead. "Spit it out, Becky! And how did scopolamine get into the mix all of a sudden? I thought we were talking previously about a dart filled with mida-something or other, and you said they were then dosed with a cocktail of DMT and baclofen."

"Midazolam—that's the pharmaceutical drug sold as Versed."

"Okay, but why is scopolamine now in this conversation? Isn't that the drug used in those seasickness patches?" Rosie asked as Vince gave her a questioning look.

"Yes, it is," confirmed Becky. "Scopolamine's now in the mix because of the tox screen results that came back on Dunn, and the hospital just sent over the test results on Mason. I expected to see the other three drugs, but there was trace evidence of scopolamine metabolites in both of their test results. Scopolamine has a half-life of four and even up to ten hours, depending on how the drug is given. It's 95% metabolized so you have to look at . . ."

"Hold on, Becky. Vince is here in the office and I'm putting you on speaker." Rosie waved Vince over to her desk, put her cell phone on speaker mode and set it on the desk between them. They leaned in close to hear over the constant buzz of squad room chatter. "Okay, Becky. Vince is here to listen to this. Now say it all again in English."

"The tests came back on both victims positive for baclofen, DMT and midazolam. I expected that, but there was scopolamine metabolite trace present also and that made me think of the perfect drug scenario."

"Which is . . .?" Rosie asked as she moved her arms in an exaggerated rolling motion to speed up Becky's explanation.

"A drug cocktail of Versed and liquid scopolamine is perfect to put a patient into what we call a twilight sleep. They could even remain upright, in sort of a sleepwalking stupor. That's how the perpetrator who did this to Dunn and Mason was able to gain access to their homes without arousing suspicion."

"Mason did say that something startled him. That could have been the window breaking so a dart gun could be used," Vince said.

"That's what I think too," Becky said. "And the broken window at Dunn's place was on the traffic side of her apartment. Street noise easily could have drowned out the glass breakage. Anyway, after the twilight stage took hold, whoever did this entered and administered another drug cocktail—intravenously this time—that contained a mix of DMT and baclofen."

"Makes sense, Becky," Vince said.

"That cocktail, in the right combination, could put someone into a comatose state that would be indistinguishable from death. The victim would be right on the verge of complete shutdown—extremely shallow breathing, the slowest heart rate that still could be considered a heartbeat, and their core would be cooling—but not so much as to stop their organ functions completely. There'd still be some minimal activity to maintain life."

Rosie and Vince were silent for a moment to consider all that the ME was saying. Vince raised an eyebrow and gestured toward the phone as he looked at Rosie and said, "That would have to be pretty specific dosing for each of our victims, Becky."

"Exactly," the ME answered. "Whoever did this to them knows a lot about drugs. Did Thomas Muñoz have a background in pharmaceuticals?"

"Not any formal training that I could find in his background, but Muñoz would probably have access to these drugs on the street," Vince said.

"Yes, these drugs have abuse potential and can be found on the black market, but I think you should be looking for someone with formal training, or . . ."

"Or what, Becky?" Rosie asked.

"It could be that whoever did this has done the same sort of thing to people before—maybe in other abductions—because it takes experience to get the dosing right to produce these specific effects."

"Like what, Becky? Like the attacker would have to know a victim's exact weight to make the dosing effective?" Vince asked.

"That would certainly help—to have an exact body weight for calculations—but a pretty good estimate of a person's weight would be fine for dose estimations. There's a little margin for error and still get the dosing in the right range. That's why I think the attacker has experience doing this sort of thing before," the ME said.

"Okay, we'll take that into consideration," Vince said.

Rosie tapped her fingers on the desk, considered everything she was hearing. She pushed the noise of the busy squad room to the background of her mind so she could focus. "So, Becky, what? They'd wake up after a certain amount of time and automatically go back home?"

"I think it's possible only with hypnosis and a hypnotic suggestion. I think while they were in the twilight sleep stage—before they were given the IV cocktail that put them into a temporary coma—Dunn and Mason were hypnotized to forget everything and programmed to return home when they woke up."

"But what woke them up, Becky?" Vince asked. "Are we still considering the theory of an implanted chip that you were talking about the other day?"

"That's really the only answer. Someone could have come into the morgue and woke up Dunn, and did the same thing at the funeral home to Mason, but I don't think that's what happened or you'd have seen that on the security cameras. The videos show only that both woke up, got dressed—one in a gown, the other in scrubs—and walked out."

"We need to access their memories with additional hypnosis. Were you able to find a hypnotist to do that?" Rosie asked.

"I did. I have appointments at San Antonio General Hospital with a hypnotherapist from their smoking cessation clinic. He's supposed to be an expert in subliminal suggestions. Your victims are scheduled to undergo hypnosis this afternoon—two o'clock for Mason and 3:30 for Dunn. After each appointment, a forensics specialist will X-ray them for an implanted chip and examine them for any puncture wound evidence."

"Great, Becky. We'll make certain both are there as scheduled," Rosie said.

Chapter 15

Sandy Dunn was having lunch with her mother when Vince called her. Sandy looked at the name listed on the caller ID, frowned and said, "Hang on, Mom. It's one of the homicide detectives. I think I should take the call." She grabbed the cloth napkin from her lap, folded it neatly next to her plate and pushed her chair back. "I'll be right back."

As she left the table and headed toward a quiet corner in the bar area of the restaurant, she answered the call. "Detective Mendez, you have a break in my abduction case?"

Vince cleared his throat. "Well, sort of. The entire tox screen panel results are back and we now know that you were drugged with several different chemicals that put you into a coma overnight."

Sandy looked around the bar area to make sure she was not being overheard. She tucked a stray stand of hair behind her ear. "I gathered that much, but what drugs and why was I targeted?"

Vince gave her the drug names and an abbreviated description of each. "The medical examiner has a theory about the order in which the drugs were given, but more importantly she thinks that the reason you and the other victim woke up with purpose and returned to your homes is that you were hypnotized while under the influence and told exactly when and how to return home."

"Hypnotized? How bizarre!"

Clearing his throat again, Vince said, "So the medical examiner thinks that if you were to undergo additional hypnosis, a good therapist might be able to latch on to some lost memories of how all this happened—and that you might even be able to recall who did this to you. We'd like your cooperation to explore that option. Would you agree to that?"

Sandy clutched the collar of her blouse in one hand and bunched up the material as she glanced toward the table where her mother sat. "I'm not sure I feel comfortable with that. We would have to agree on specific questions the therapist could ask."

"I'm sure that could be worked out. We're not trying to pry into your personal life or anything like that, but I'm sure the therapist would like to pursue whatever path will guide him to understand the events of the night we thought you died."

"I realize that, Detective, and I want to get to the bottom of this crime as much as you do. I simply won't allow the therapist to ask questions that relate to my clients or to my law practice in any way. I'm firm on that. If we can agree on that point, I'm happy to cooperate."

"That's good news and I'm sure we can guarantee that, but there's one other thing that we need your permission for. The ME also thinks that maybe there's a chip implanted in you that emitted an electrical impulse the morning you walked out of the morgue. She thinks this chip actually woke you up."

Sandy laughed so loud that the bartender looked her way. She glanced toward him and immediately looked down to the floor and cupped her phone into one hand and spoke more softly. "Detective, you've got to be joking. A chip? In me . . . still in me? How is that possible? I would have noticed . . . or the doctors would have noticed when I was examined at the hospital after all this happened . . . wouldn't they?"

"I'm sorry. I simply don't have those answers and that's why we want your permission to do a full body X-ray. I'm told it'll be minimally invasive and that it could help explain how you woke up. We'd like you to agree to allow us to do the X-ray."

There was silence on the line while Sandy decided. Vince did not interrupt the quiet while she thought through her decision. Finally, she sighed heavily into the phone and said, "Detective, I agree. I'd be lying if I said that this event . . . whatever it is that happened to me . . . isn't bothering me. I need answers and if this is the way to get them, then I'm all in. When and where will we do this?"

Vince gave her specifics regarding the scheduled appointments and she hung up. As she headed back to the table, she noticed that her mother's eyes were red and puffy. Sandy sat and stared at her mother for a moment before either of them spoke.

Using her napkin to dab at her eyes, Sandy's mother said, "I guess that call from a detective reminded me of all that you've been through. I'm sorry to make such a spectacle of myself." She turned her head slightly to glance around the room.

Sandy put a hand on her mother's shoulder. "It's okay, Mom. The police gave me some good news. They may have found a way to discover who did this. They think I was hypnotized to wake up from a drug induced coma and was programmed to go back home like I did."

"They want to hypnotize you? Maybe take you back to childhood memories? That sort of thing?"

"No, not that kind of therapy session. I understand it's a special process to uncover more recent repressed memories, those that are connected to the night everyone thought I died." She gazed at her mother and was surprised to see a familiar expression on her mother's face, the same look of fear that she often saw in the faces of clients who suddenly realized that their cases were going south and that they would probably end up in prison.

Sandy began to fidget with the napkin she had folded to one side of her plate before taking the detective's call. She stared at her mother for a moment longer. "Mom, why did you bring up my childhood just now when I mentioned hypnotherapy? Is there something bothering you, something you're afraid I might remember from when I was a child?"

Her mother giggled a nervous laugh. "Of course not. I'm only worried about your emotional state. I'm concerned how dredging up the memory of that awful night will affect you. I don't think you should go through with it. There has to be some other way the police can investigate this case."

"Mother, it's more than that. I see it in your face. You're concerned about something that might come out in the therapy session, but I can't imagine what that might be."

"Nonsense! You've switched into lawyer mode and I don't appreciate being cross-examined." Dolores Dunn lifted an eyebrow and folded her arms across her chest.

Sandy reached out to touch her mother's shoulder but she resisted and turned her head away from Sandy. "Mom, you gave me a wonderful childhood and great memories. What makes you so afraid of me undergoing hypnosis?"

"Don't be ridiculous, Sandy. I'm only concerned about you and this horrible experience you went through. Now finish your lunch so we can order dessert."

Rosie walked up to Vince's desk with two steaming cups of coffee. She handed one to him, took a sip from the other and asked, "So how did your visit with Sandy Dunn go? Did she agree to the appointments at the hospital clinic?"

"She was reluctant at first and surprised that we believe there's an electronic chip in her, but she eventually warmed up to the idea of hypnosis and X-rays. She agreed to it all. How'd it go with Gerry Mason?"

"Not as well. Gerry resisted a return to the hospital . . . reiterated the familiar phrase that patients go there to die. We bantered back and forth for some time before he finally gave in. I convinced him that it was in his best interest and possibly the only way to arrive at the truth, and I had to promise that there would be no overnight stay involved. He had a hard time disagreeing with any of that, although he tried his best to be a royal pain about it all."

Vince chuckled. "Listen, remember when I said I talked to that warden about a couple of other inmates who were chummy with Shapiro and Muñoz while they were in prison?"

"Yes, you said they were all on kitchen duty together—model prisoners—and that one of them turned up as a current employee of the Shapiro Gallery." Rosie lifted her coffee to her lips and took a sip.

"That's Angel Moreno, the guy who has a history of being around death a lot but always escaped any major indictments. We'll need to dig into his life some more, but I have the background on that other inmate now," Vince said.

"Great. Hopefully it's something that ties Shapiro and Angel Moreno to the abductions and murders."

Vince smiled as he stood, set his coffee on the desk and walked to the evidence board that had been pushed into a corner of the squad room. He rolled it away from the wall and arranged it in front of their desks. He pointed to three pictures taped to the board—Shapiro, Muñoz and then at Moreno's photo between the other two. "One more picture goes here next to Moreno." He stepped back to his desk, pulled a photo from the top of a folder, grabbed a black marker and moved back to the board. He taped the photo to the board under Moreno's and drew arrows from that picture to those of Moreno, Muñoz and Shapiro. Next he tapped the knuckle of his index finger on the new photo.

"This guy is Alejandro Rojas, Alex to his friends. He served his time, got out of prison and eventually fulfilled his parole obligations. That's when he was allowed to move to Cartagena, Columbia and went into the toy importing business."

Rosie was about to take another sip from her cup but stopped with the cup midway to her lips. "Toys? Samuel Jennings had a toy store. Are those two connected?"

"Financial records on Jennings indicate that he shipped a lot of a certain kind of science kit to Cartagena right after Rojas got there. It went on for about a year."

"What kind of kit?"

Vince walked to his desk and pulled copies of shipping documents from the evidence folder. He handed them to Rosie.

She put her cup down and studied the documents. As she read, her mouth eased into a grin. "Jennings shipped Ant Farm Science Kits on a regular basis to Colombia. Where is this toy manufacturer?"

Vince smiled, grabbed his coffee and gulped down a big swallow as Rosie gazed again at the printouts. "Fort Worth, Texas. But that doesn't matter, Rosie, not even the type of toys shipped. What matters is that when Rojas got to Cartagena, Jennings exported toys to him. The problem is that the financials don't add up. Jennings shipped more toys than Rojas ever sold. In fact, I could only find a small money trail of Rojas selling a few toys to one tourist retailer."

Rosie squinted and shrugged. "So Jennings did business with this guy, and maybe it's a shady business deal—or deals—under the table for cash. But what's that got to do with Shapiro and these murders?"

"Everything!"

"Are you saying Jennings was murdered because he knew Rojas?"

"I'm pretty sure, and it's because of one important reason." Vince turned, walked back to the evidence board and tapped on the picture of Rojas. "After Jennings stopped exporting those toys, Rojas switched to art dealing. He started importing Shapiro's gallery paintings into Colombia." Vince took one last swallow of coffee and set it down on his desk. He took the marking pen, wrote the word "paintings" next to Shapiro's picture and drew a line from Shapiro's photo to that of Rojas.

Rosie's eyes widened. "Okay, now we're getting somewhere. Is it Mason's paintings Shapiro sent over there?"

"When Shapiro began featuring Mason's paintings in the gallery, much of that art was sold and shipped offshore."

Rosie walked up to the board and pointed to Shapiro's picture while she asked, "Interesting. Can we link his shipments to the art dealing business owned by Rojas?"

"Yes, I have Shapiro's export records to an art gallery in Cartagena owned by Rojas." Vince moved to his desk, pulled records from the folder and returned to the board. He handed several printouts to Rosie.

She looked over the documents and finally touched a finger in succession to the pictures of Shapiro, Muñoz and Rojas on the evidence board. "So what's the connection? Forged art again?" She stepped back, shrugged and folded her arms. "But we already have an artist—Gerry Mason—and he's legit. How does it all fit?"

Vince pointed a finger at her. "That's the question! And that's what puzzled me until I dug deeper. Just like with those toy shipments from Jennings, there are some missing paintings in the equation."

"Come again?"

Vince smiled and nodded toward his desk. "I've got import records for twice as many paintings shipped to Rojas than I have in payments to Mason."

"How do you know that? The value could have been inflated for insurance purposes, or whatever, on those shipments."

"No, Rosie, I get that the value of a painting may vary depending on size, subject matter and things like that. What I'm referring to is that

Shapiro's invoices show payments to Mason for exactly half as many paintings as Rojas received."

"But . . ."

Vince pointed at Rosie again. "Don't you get it? All those paintings were supposedly painted by Gerry Mason, only some weren't."

"So this must be where Thomas Muñoz comes into the picture?"

"That's what I think. Remember, Muñoz and Jennings were friends," Vince said.

Rosie thought back to her conversation with Mason the night she visited with him at the hospital. "That's right. Mason mentioned that Jennings introduced him to Muñoz."

Vince looked over at Rosie's empty cup and said, "Get us a couple of fresh brews and I'll walk you through the link between Jennings and Muñoz."

Rosie took the empty cups, sauntered to the break room and poured the last of a pot into the cups. She joked around with a couple of other detectives who were seated at the table having a snack, told them it was their turn to make a fresh pot before they left the room or she'd see to it that they'd be demoted to uniforms and squad car patrols again.

When she returned to her desk, she set her cup on the desk and handed the other steaming brew to Vince. He said, "Thanks, you'll need a kick of caffeine to follow my theory."

He glanced at the board and pointed to the pictures of Muñoz and Jennings. "They were neighbors once. That was a long time ago, before Jennings and Mason moved in together."

Rosie smirked and waved a hand at the evidence board. "I was wondering how Jennings knew Muñoz."

"That's the link—something as innocent as chummy neighbors."

Rosie chuckled. "So . . . because Jennings was an old friend of Muñoz—who was probably restoring art, or maybe forging art for Shapiro—Mason eventually connected with Shapiro?"

"Yes, I think this all started because of Muñoz's friendship with Jennings," Vince said.

Rosie's eyes grew wide as she connected the dots. "And . . . that's when Shapiro started shipping paintings to Rojas . . . after Mason consigned his work to Shapiro's gallery?"

"I think so," Vince said. He turned to the board and studied the pictures taped to it one more time before glancing around the room as if deep in thought. Finally, he twisted back to Rosie with a frown on his face. "The question we need to answer is if it's simple art forgery—with Muñoz duplicating some of Mason's work—or is there more involved?"

"Smuggling something out of the country would explain why Shapiro would need more paintings to ship than Mason could continue to paint, more paintings mean more smuggling opportunities." She took the marking pen from Vince's hand and turned toward the board. She wrote the names Jennings and Mason next to Shapiro's picture. She added a question mark behind each name. "I can't see either Jennings or Mason being involved in a smuggling scheme, though."

"But Jennings knew Muñoz, who got Shapiro and Mason to do business together. And Jennings shipped Ant Farm Kits to Columbia before the art shipments began—toys that could easily hide whatever they smuggled into Columbia," Vince reminded Rosie.

She smiled and nodded. "The kind of toys that customs officers might not want to inspect very closely."

"Right. Who would want to inspect an ant farm and chance letting those things loose?"

"But what could they be smuggling—drugs? And why smuggle them out of the country? That doesn't make sense." She gave Vince a puzzled look.

"I'm pretty sure those paintings—fake and real, and the toys before that—are being used to hide something that's being sent to South America. The question is what?"

Rosie went back to her desk and flopped into her chair. She tapped her fingers on the desk before saying, "That's why we need to dig into what's going on with Shapiro and Moreno at that art gallery."

Vince glanced at the clock hanging on the wall across the squad room. "Agreed, but first we need to head to the hospital. It's about time for Dunn and Mason to have their hypnotherapy sessions.

Chapter 16

The hypnotherapist invited Sandy Dunn to sit in a comfortable lounge chair in his dimly lit, monochromatic office. He smiled and explained that he would be using the Ericksonian hypnotherapy process to clear her mind of the present, relax her muscles to free tension and reduce nerve impulses, and that he would guide her mind to release memories of the night in question by giving specific suggestions and gentle guided commands.

As he had done with Gerry Mason earlier in the afternoon, the therapist asked Sandy if she had any questions about the session before they started. She nodded that she did and asked, "Doctor, what makes Ericksonian Hypnosis different from other forms of hypnotic trances?"

"That's an excellent question, Sandy. Other forms of hypnosis actually do put you in a trance, or more specifically take you out of your 'everyday trance' to cause a change in behavior. That's what I do to stop people from smoking. I command them with direct suggestions to move away from certain everyday rituals—like smoking—and I create new rituals for them that help eliminate the bad habits."

"But we're not changing habits today, Doctor. We're trying to get me to remember something I don't seem able to. How will you do that?"

"In a way, Sandy, that's a habit also—the habit, or obsession, of repressing distasteful memories. Ericksonian Hypnosis takes a different approach from traditional hypnosis. It works by using indirect rather than direct suggestion. Indirect suggestions are much harder for the conscious mind to resist because they're not usually recognized as suggestions at all. The gentle prodding of the relaxed mind often produces submission and allows guided imagery to release lost memories."

When Sandy said that she understood and was ready to begin, the therapist secured her written permission to tape the session, reclined her chair into a comfortable position and immediately led her through a series of relaxation exercises. Before she realized what was happening, he had placed her under a deep, yet controlled, hypnosis. It had taken him several minutes longer to bring Gerry Mason to the same hypnotic state during his session and considerably more discussion to convince him to sign the waiver before the session could begin.

The therapist focused on Sandy and issued soft-spoken commands utilizing metaphors to distract her mind from blocking memories based on previous direct hypnotic suggestions. He asked Sandy to go back in time to a favorite moment in her childhood when she had felt completely safe and secure. He suggested that she continue to remember that comfortable feeling as she thought about the evening her mother was coming over for dinner.

He asked her if she was happy that her mother was coming to visit and Sandy responded with a broad smile. At that point, specific questions from the therapist freed Sandy's mind so she could speak of her experiences the day she was drugged.

Sandy appeared to be awake but her eyes were closed as she remembered and calmly told of her abduction. "I feel a prickling in my lower shoulder, like someone accidently stuck a thumbtack into me. I try to reach for it but can't control my arms. They float in mid-air."

She hesitated a moment. The therapist knew she was reliving the night in her mind, just as Mason had done during his session. The hypnotist gave her a moment to mentally replay the events before asking, "What are you seeing now?"

"I can't move. I'm sitting in my chair but feel like I'm hovering a few inches above it."

The therapist moved closer to the edge of his seat and gripped his notepad tightly. He realized that Sandy was recalling the initial effects of the drug-induced twilight sleep administered by the dart. "What happens next, Sandy?"

"Someone is pulling me out of the chair. No, that's not it. He's removing my shoe and I slip down a little in my chair. Now I see a type of gun, like the ones they use to inject capsules under someone's skin."

The therapist sat straighter and jotted down words onto his yellow, lined pad. He asked gently, "Who is with you? A man or a woman?"

"A man."

"Look at the gun again," the therapist suggested. "Is he injecting something into you?"

"I think so. It's under the fold of my big toe. It buzzed my toe the next morning, made it shake. I woke up."

The therapist wrote a few notes and gazed around his office. He glanced toward the plants that filled one corner of his office, the only color in the room other than shades of gray. He made a mental note to water them later. He sat back in his chair, thought about what to ask next. So far, Sandy's responses were very similar to Gerry Mason's.

"Let's talk about what happened after you woke up, after your toe buzzed. What did you do when you felt your toe vibrate?"

"I did what I was supposed to."

"What were you supposed to do, Sandy? It's okay to tell me."

The therapist tilted his head and studied Sandy. She remained relaxed in her reclined chair, so he asked, "What do you do when you wake up?"

"I need to find something to wear. I . . . I'm naked. There are scrubs on a hook near a shelf . . . clothes like medical students wear. I put the top and bottoms on before looking for an outside door. It's down the hall and unlocked."

"Do you go down the hall?"

"Yes, and I go outside and wait for the blue car to arrive."

The therapist suggested, "That car has now arrived. Do you see it?"

"It drove up as soon as I got to the curb."

"What happens next? What does the driver do at this point?"

"He waits in the car. I wonder if I should wait at the curb or go to the car."

"Can you describe the car?" the therapist asked.

"A dark blue sedan, four doors, mid-sized. There's a man behind the wheel. I'm supposed to wait for him."

The therapist observed his patient closely to make sure she remained calm. He understood that an unpleasant memory could upset her and block further disclosure. Sandy appeared relaxed, her body molded into the curve of the recliner. He asked her to continue.

"The driver gets out of the car, he walks up to me, takes me by the hand and leads me to the back seat of the car. I lie down across the seat. He says that's how I have to ride in the blue car."

"Did the man drive you somewhere once you were in the back seat?"

"Home, he took me home. I'm happy to be home. I'm supposed to continue what I was doing before."

"And what was that, Sandy? What are you doing now?"

"I go into my apartment, find clothes similar to what I had on before the man injected my toe with the buzzing thing. And I continue to prepare for my mother coming over for dinner."

The therapist noticed a frown developing on Sandy's brow. He said, "It's okay, Sandy. Nothing can hurt you now. You're safe here with me, safe to remember what you couldn't before."

"But he told me not to tell anyone. I'm sorry. You should forget all this."

The therapist reached out to touch her hand but stopped short of any contact, realizing that any external stimuli could derail a successful hypnotic process. Instead, he said, "It's all right to tell me, Sandy. You did what the man asked of you. The memory was forgotten, exactly as he suggested. You did precisely what he asked, so now it's okay to remember those things and tell me about them. Do you understand that it's *now okay* to remember what you forgot?"

"Yes, I understand, but I can't tell you about the shipments. He said never to talk about those to anyone."

The therapist could not resist a smile. The session was proceeding well, even better than expected. He understood, however, that asking a wrong question could agitate his patient and end the session at any moment. He referred to his notes before continuing and noted that Sandy's memories continued to mirror those of Gerry Mason's experience.

"Remember, you are safe with me. What about the shipments? What does the man want you to forget about them?"

"I'm afraid of what will happen if I talk about them. I can't remember. I won't remember!"

"Sandy, memories are in the past. They can't harm you in the present. You are safe with me and it's okay now to remember, even things you were told to forget. It's okay to tell me."

"It's something about how many paintings are being sent to South America. I don't understand. He wants me to forget, but I don't remember what I'm supposed to forget."

Sandy's face took on a troubled look. She frowned, her forehead creased and her lips pinched together.

The therapist frowned also, tapped his pen on the notepad in his lap and took a moment to decide if he should push Sandy further. He decided against it. "It's okay, Sandy. You don't have to remember anything you don't want to. Now I'd like you to go back to the time just *after* the man injected your toe with the thing that woke you the next morning."

He noticed that the frown on Sandy's forehead remained. In a gentle voice, the therapist said, "I'm there with you, Sandy. No harm will come to you as long as *I'm* there with you. Do you understand that and trust me?"

Sandy smiled. "Yes, I do."

The therapist took in a deep, cleansing breath. He let it out and asked, "Can you see the man's face? Can you describe him?"

"Yes, he looks determined, busy, methodical. He has a scowl on his face."

"The man can't hurt you now. Remember that. Tell me what he looks like."

"Very masculine, powerful arms, calm and controlled manner."

"Do you recognize the person?"

"No, not the one who injected me. I've never seen him before, but I recognize the other man with him."

"There's a second man in the room?"

"Yes, it's Angel."

The therapist smiled. This was new information. Gerry Mason could not identify his assailant and had only mentioned that there was one man present in his house. "Where do you know Angel from?"

"He works for Mr. Shapiro, my client. He's Shapiro's special assistant."

The therapist again sat on the edge of his chair. He inhaled deeply, let the air out slowly and quietly through his nose and willed his pulse back to normal. "Sandy, we're still at the time when the man injected your big toe with something that buzzed the next morning. Can you tell me what he does after that?"

"He's lifting my arm, rolls up a sleeve and feels around. I think . . . he's looking for a vein, like a nurse would do if I gave blood."

"Does he find a vein?"

"Only after he puts a thick, rubber band around my upper arm."

"And where is Angel while the man is doing this to your arm?"

"He's just watching, making sure the man doesn't hurt me. He asks the man to be gentle with me."

The therapist studied Sandy's face for signs of tension. She seemed to remain relaxed, so he pushed on. "What do you feel next?"

Clenching one fist, Sandy arched her back in the lounger. The therapist said, "I'm with you and remember you can't be harmed when I'm with you. This is *only a memory* of what happened. You can remember without feeling threatened. Do you understand?"

"Yes," Sandy said as she relaxed into the cushion of the reclined chair, her arms limp at her side.

"You can tell me what happens. You won't be harmed."

Sandy nodded and continued. "The man removes a large syringe from a bag and sticks the needle into my arm."

The therapist furrowed his brow and quickly referred to his earlier notes from Mason's session. He had noted that Gerry Mason remembered a man giving him suggestions—commands actually—regarding what he should do when he woke up. According to Gerry, that happened just before the man found a vein and gave the bolus of the drug cocktail that put him to sleep. There was definitely no mention of a second man present.

The hypnotherapist put Gerry's session notes aside and asked, "Did something happen before the man administered the liquid from the syringe?"

Sandy shook her head slowly side to side. "It doesn't hurt when he pushes all the liquid into my vein."

She hesitated at that point and grimaced.

"What is it, Sandy?"

"Darkness. I see darkness and nothing else until my toe buzzes."

When they were taken out of their hypnotic trances, Mason and Dunn woke up feeling as if nothing had happened. The hypnosis of Mason had produced similar results to the session with Dunn, only Mason could not identify his attacker but he did remember what the man looked like and described him. Mason also remembered that he was given certain commands to do things after waking up. Sandy Dunn recalled nothing about that prior to being knocked out.

After reporting the results of each therapy session to the detectives and the medical examiner, the hypnotherapist ended his comments with, "One final thing that troubled me and which was common with each of your victims is that the hypnotic suggestions included one that confused both of them.

Rosie and Vince frowned in unison and glanced toward each other briefly before Rosie asked the therapist, "Did you discover what that suggestion was?"

"They were commanded to forget what they heard about some shipments of paintings. Each said that they didn't understand what they were supposed to forget, but that the suggestion seemed important to their attacker and the thought of speaking about those shipments made both Dunn and Mason visibly afraid."

When the briefing ended, both detectives thanked the therapist for his time and expertise and Vince walked him to the door.

After Mason and Dunn had completed their hypnosis, each underwent an extensive physical exam and X-rays by the medical examiner and a forensics associate. Special attention was given to examining their toes and arms. Miniature chips an eighth of an inch long, and about half as wide, were found under the skin on the bottom of each patient's big left toe.

The chips were removed and sent to the crime lab for analysis. A remaining puncture mark, not quite healed, was found on the inside of Mason's right elbow—in the antecubital area. No corresponding puncture mark was found on Dunn's arm.

After the victims were ushered into a private waiting area to await conclusive results of their therapy sessions and exams, Becky spoke more extensively about the results to Rosie and Vince in a small conference room on the other side of the hospital hallway.

"The puncture mark on Dunn probably has already healed," Becky said. "I couldn't find an entry spot for the drug cocktail that caused the comatose state. But I did find a wound on her upper back from the dart. That produced a jagged edge as it hit and there's still evidence of tissue damage in that area."

"What about Mason?" Rosie asked.

"We found the same type of irregular wound on his back. Small and not enough to bother him, but it was consistent with a dart puncture that hadn't completely healed. The injection site on his arm could have been from the drug injection or it could be from an injection site used by the hospital when he had his pacemaker replaced. I can't be sure."

"The results of the hypnosis are pretty conclusive," Vince said. "Both describe similar events and in the same general order. Dunn states that her attacker is a man that she did not recognize but confirms that Angel Moreno was in the room also. Mason describes his attacker as someone who looks like Dunn's attacker, but says that man was the only one in the room."

Rosie held up her phone. It displayed a prison photo of Muñoz. "Mason's description sounds a lot like how Dunn described this man. Could he have been working on orders from Angel Moreno?"

"Could be. Muñoz is the obvious attacker since he had the drugs and all that hypnosis information at his house and he fits the description, but why did Moreno personally supervise Dunn's attack and not Mason's?" Vince asked.

"Good question, and another puzzling piece of information," Rosie said.

Becky nodded. "The hypnotherapist thinks both were subjected to Traditional Suggestion Hypnosis, a process that puts post-hypnotic suggestions directly into a person's subconscious. The therapist said it's easier for a non-clinician to use that method. It's quick, simple and effective—particularly when the patient is already under the influence of drugs."

"Will Dunn or Mason remember today's hypnotic session?" Vince asked.

"No, the therapist's job was only to get at the raw truth. If they had come out of this hypnotic experience remembering all that happened, the therapist thought he'd have to help them deal with the confusion and fear such knowledge would bring. That's for another clinician to deal with at a later date. It's better now that neither will remember anything about today's sessions," Becky explained.

"Could we show them a picture of Muñoz to confirm that he was their attacker?" Rosie asked.

"The therapist said that it would not be wise, that it might bring up disturbing memories. I'd go with the descriptive evidence for now and save the photo until later," Becky advised.

Rosie nodded. "Okay, we'll work with that plan for now, especially since the primary attacker is dead." Vince shrugged his shoulders in agreement.

Becky looked across the hall, through a glass window and into the private waiting area. She sighed as she turned back to Rosie and pushed her chin toward the waiting room. "So what do we say about today? They're waiting to hear what happened to them and who's responsible."

"We need to round up Angel Moreno before we say anything. We think Moreno murdered Jennings and Muñoz, but we need more evidence to prove that and also have to figure out how Shapiro fits into this puzzle."

Rosie glanced at Vince. She raked fingers through her hair and bit her lower lip before asking,

"Got any ideas how we tell our two victims that they only *dreamed* about being dead?"

Vince chuckled. "So a 'dream' is what you want to call it? That's how we explain a lunatic turning those two into puppets for some unknown scheme?"

"That's about right, partner. You have a better idea?"

Vince shrugged. "Why don't we keep it simple? Let's tell them we know the type of drugs that knocked them out and that a little electronic thing was implanted in their foot and that's what woke them from a trance. We say there are vague leads on the rest and leave it at that."

Rosie looked at Vince like he had grown a third arm. "Good luck with that. Like any good lawyer Dunn will fire back twenty questions in a heartbeat. And cranky old man Mason should be about as congenial as Dunn with *that* doublespeak."

Chapter 17

Before leaving the hospital, Rosie met with Gerry Mason while Vince did the same with Sandy Dunn. They explained, with as little detail as possible, how each was drugged and put into a comatose state that made it seem like they had died. They fielded the expected questions with little more than that they were working on finding who was responsible and why they had become victims.

Sandy surprised both detectives when she remained calm and expressionless. She said, "I'm going to trust that you'll do all you can to close this case. For now, I'm satisfied that the investigation's being handled in an orderly manner." She left the hospital without further discussion.

Gerry, however, ranted on about being a victim. He put a hand on one hip and waved the other hand through the air. "My life's been turned upside down, violated in unspeakable ways and all you give me is 'we're working on it'? Really? You have to do more!"

Rosie looked to the side and let out a sigh before focusing back on Mason. "Gerry, things take time. I appreciate your coming in and allowing us to examine you. We now know about the chip, and other things."

He jutted out his jaw, grimaced and pointed a finger to within inches of Rosie's nose. "What other things? I know I must have said something important under hypnosis. I can see it in your face, but you're hiding it from me. Why?"

"We're not hiding anything. We're investigating. We have clues, but no actual answers yet. You have to be patient and let us do our job."

"Your job is to protect me and I don't feel safe. What if something like . . . like what happened before happens again?"

"You mean your pacemaker?"

Mason looked around to make sure he could not be overheard. He whispered, "No, what if I die again, *but come back again*? Have you considered that?"

"Look, Gerry, we don't think that's a possibility anymore."

"Why? That means you must know more than what you're saying. Tell me!"

Rosie closed her fists and punched her thighs. Through clenched teeth she said, "If you don't go home this instant, Gerry, I swear . . ." She took a deep breath, managed a forced smile and altered her approach. "Gerry, do me a favor. Go home and let us get back to work. Okay?"

Mason raised an eyebrow, turned on his heels and walked down the hall without another word. He turned once and pointed a finger at Rosie, but he never spoke. After a moment, he spun around again and continued walking toward the elevators.

When the detectives finally left the hospital, they decided to pay a visit to the Shapiro Gallery. They arrived late in the afternoon and parked in the lot at the side of the building. There were three other cars parked there. A quick check of the license plates through the Department of Motor Vehicles revealed that two of the more expensive cars were leased to the gallery. Someone named Betty Moore owned the third.

The detectives strolled to the building's entrance and opened the door. Cool, dry air brushed past them as they entered. They walked through the lobby to the art display area and found a mature woman dressed in business attire. She was sitting at a desk near a corner of the room.

She stood, smiled and approached the detectives. "Good afternoon. Could I be of assistance?"

"Are you Ms. Moore?" Rosie asked.

The woman put a hand to her throat. "Have we met before?"

Rosie showed her badge. "I'm Detective Young and this is my partner Detective Mendez. A name came up in a case we're investigating. Do you know Angel Moreno?"

Ms. Moore's left eyebrow lifted slightly. "Yes, he works for Mr. Shapiro, the gallery owner. What's this about?"

"What type of job does Mr. Moreno do here?"

Standing straighter than before, as if on alert, Ms. Moore said, "He works for Mr. Shapiro, not particularly for the gallery. He's . . . he's Mr. Shapiro's personal assistant . . . sort of an aide."

"Like a medical aide?" Vince asked.

She clenched her hand. "No, not that kind. He's more like a . . . a go-to guy, a right-hand man. I can't really—"

"Is he here now?" Rosie asked.

The woman looked over her shoulder, toward the elevator. "He's upstairs with Mr. Shapiro. There's an important shipment . . . I mean, they're working on a client's order."

"A shipment of paintings?" Vince asked.

She turned to Vince and raised that same eyebrow slightly higher than before. It caused her forehead to crease. "You really should see Mr. Shapiro about that."

"Do you have a warehouse area? Are the paintings being prepared for shipment now?"

"Yes . . . I mean . . . you should speak with Mr. Shapiro." Her face flushed.

"May we see where your paintings are crated for shipping?"

She relaxed her posture and pasted a smile on her face. "I'm sure Mr. Shapiro would love to give you a personal tour."

Rosie touched Vince's arm and gestured toward the front door. "That won't be necessary. We appreciate your time."

A feeble "thank you" escaped from Ms. Moore's lips as the detectives exited the gallery.

When they were outside, Vince turned to Rosie, frowned and pointed back at the building. "What was that all about?"

"You heard the lady. They're preparing a shipment of paintings. Let's pull the car around, park down the block a little and see what happens."

"A stakeout? But it could take hours before anything happens. Or who knows, it may not even be today."

"That's okay, Vince. It'll give us time to get a warrant to search that shipment. We suspect drugs are hiding in those paintings. Given the criminal history of the players involved, a search warrant would be easy to secure. Whatever's in the paintings could be central to our murder cases and to solving the abductions of Dunn and Mason."

Vince nodded. "Good plan. I'll call the station to initiate one and contact our favorite judge. A uniform can get it signed and it'll be in our hands within a couple of hours."

Rosie shrugged and rubbed the back of her neck. "In the meantime, we wait. I could sure use a cup of coffee about now, though. Get a uniform to send over some with the warrant."

Chapter 18

In a little over two hours, the search warrant, along with coffee and sandwiches, arrived via a plain-clothes patrolman in an unmarked black sedan. Rosie and Vince waited another two hours in their vehicle with no noticeable activity around the gallery—no customers and no shipping truck to pick up anything. The only exception was Ms. Moore, who left the art gallery in her car at closing time.

Dusk turned into darkness and the air grew still. Several people strolled past as they walked dogs through the quiet neighborhood lined with vintage, restored homes in the near downtown area.

Rosie heard crickets begin their evening litany and hit the steering wheel with the palm of her hand. "That's it. Let's get a plain-clothes pair to relieve us. It's getting late and I'm done waiting."

"Not so fast," Vince said, and pointed in the direction of the gallery. A man fitting the description of Angel Moreno exited the front door, locked it with a key and walked around the brick building to the rear parking area. Several minutes later a luxury SUV came around the back of the building toward the street with Moreno behind the wheel.

Rosie started her car, hit the switch for an emergency light bar imbedded in the car's front grill and raced down the street to the gallery parking lot. She blocked the entrance to the street and both detectives jumped from their car shouting, "Police. Exit the vehicle with your hands up."

Moreno, stunned for the moment, did nothing.

Rosie repeated her command more slowly the second time, her words several decibels louder than before. "I said exit your vehicle with your hands up."

For a moment longer, the man remained seated behind the wheel. Unhurriedly, he held up one hand, opened the driver's door with his other and exited the car. He stood up straight, put both hands behind his head, laced his fingers together and remained in place with elbows up and out. He appeared calm and looked directly ahead.

"Seems to know the drill," Vince said.

The detectives approached the man inches at a time, their guns drawn. Rosie asked, "Where are the paintings?"

Moreno nodded toward the detectives. "Hey, what's goin' on?" When Rosie aimed her weapon at the man's face, he shut up and pushed his chin toward the rear of the SUV. "In the back."

"We have a search warrant. Is there anything inside other than paintings?" Rosie asked.

The man shrugged. "All I do is drive."

"Where are you taking those paintings?" Vince asked.

"To a private air field, Stinson Municipal. What are ya' busting me for?"

"Is your boss inside?"

Moreno sighed at Vince. "I drive. That's my job."

Vince kept his weapon pointed at the man, but he glanced toward Rosie. "I'll take a look inside." He holstered his gun, moved to the back of the vehicle and opened the rear doors. There were three stacks of thin rectangular crates, four per stack. He pulled out one from the top of the closest stack, unscrewed the winged hinges on each of the four corners and removed the front of the crate. Nestled inside was an impressionistic oil painting in a frame almost the exact size of the inner dimensions of the crate.

He removed the framed painting and examined it. He frowned when he shook the canvas up and down, and called out to Rosie. "This painting is really heavy and way too thick." He examined the piece of art more closely, held it up to the streetlight and turned the frame sideways. "The back of this canvas is as thick as the frame."

Rosie turned to Moreno. "Keep your hands up where I can see them. Who were you meeting at Stinson?"

Moreno let his elbows drop down, but he held his hands up and in full view of the detectives. "I don't know. I'm meetin' a jet there, some bigwig . . ."

Vince punched the canvas with a knuckle. "Something's between the painting and a false canvas back. Maybe it's drugs, like we were thinking." He took out a pocketknife and cut along three sides at the back of the frame. Stacks of cash spilled out onto the ground."

"Holy shit! It's not drugs. It's money."

Rosie took her eyes off Moreno for a second to glance at Vince. Moreno noticed and took off sprinting toward the front of the building. He raced around the corner before Rosie could react. She ran after him.

Vince dropped the painting, pulled out his weapon and followed his partner. When he turned the corner of the building, he saw Rosie slipping into the gallery's front door, apparently chasing after Moreno. Vince did the same and once inside he realized the interior lights were off. He closed the door behind him to prevent being silhouetted in the doorframe and made into an easy target.

He advanced a couple of feet into the room and bumped into Rosie. He whispered, "Where is he?"

"I don't know. I saw him unlock the door and slip in, but I lost him in the dark."

"Is he armed?" Vince asked.

"We didn't get that far. Move left, away from the door. Did you see any light switches earlier?"

"Didn't notice. I'll go right. You stay left," Vince said.

"No. We'd be in each other's line of fire."

Vince sighed nervously. "Then you come up with a plan."

Rosie's eyes were growing accustomed to the darkness. She saw the illuminated elevator buttons across the room and the exit sign hanging from the ceiling near the back door. There was a dim light in one corner of the room. She remembered seeing Ms. Moore at her desk earlier and realized it was the glow of the computer screen on Moore's desk.

As she focused on the corner, a shadow passed in front of the lit screen. She fired slightly left of the desk where the person crossed and heard the crack of wood. The bullet splintered the edge of the desk. She touched Vince's shoulder, pushing him deeper into the room and followed.

Suddenly the front door opened. "Hello?" a female voice called out. A light switch clicked on and Sandy Dunn stared at both detectives. She shrieked and Vince pointed his gun at her. Rosie kept hers in the direction of the desk.

Dunn screamed, "Don't shoot." Vince lowered his weapon.

Rosie saw Angel Moreno crouched in a corner behind the desk. She shouted, "Hands up, Moreno."

Moreno stood but remained behind the desk. A Glock semi-automatic was in his hand. As if in slow motion, he placed the weapon on the desk, raised his hands behind his head and laced his fingers together.

Rosie approached him. Before she could walk the distance to the desk, however, she heard a scream behind her. She turned to see Seth Shapiro grab Dunn around the neck, placing her in front of him like a shield.

Vince raised his weapon and aimed at Shapiro, who pointed a gun back at him.

Rosie spun around in time to see Moreno grab for his Glock. "Not so fast, Moreno. Touch that weapon and you'll regret it," she said.

Moreno froze in place, his hand hovering over the gun on the desk. He locked eyes with Rosie's. She smiled. "Think I'm bluffing? Try me!"

No one spoke and no one moved for several seconds. Finally, Shapiro broke the silence. "Sandy, I'm not going to hurt you unless they force me to."

He pulled Dunn backwards toward the door. She stumbled as Shapiro gripped her more tightly around the neck. He dragged her slowly. She tripped again and screamed.

Rosie jerked her head in the direction of the scream only for a moment, but that was enough for Moreno to grab his gun from the desk and fire.

Rosie thought she had been hit and spun around to shoot back. Before she pulled the trigger, however, Moreno threw down his weapon and pushed his hands high into the air. Rosie took her finger off the trigger, a confused look on her face. She ran up to Moreno, gun pointed directly at him, and kicked his weapon under the desk.

She twisted her head and called out, "Vince?" and saw him running to Shapiro.

Dunn was on her knees crying, Shapiro was lying on the ground holding his bloody shoulder. Vince kicked Shapiro's weapon across the floor.

Rosie turned back to Moreno, told him to lie on the floor with his hands behind his back. She cuffed him and yelled, "Vince, you okay?"

"I'm fine, but Shapiro's losing a lot of blood. Call for an ambulance. I'll apply pressure to stop the bleeding."

After calling for backup and medical support, Rosie leaned closer to Moreno. He remained face down on the ground and offered no resistance. She asked, "You shot your boss?"

Almost in a whisper, he said, "He was going to hurt Sandy. I couldn't let that happen."

Chapter 19

Shapiro was transported to the hospital. He underwent emergency surgery to remove the bullet and to repair a torn artery in his shoulder. Angel Moreno was placed under arrest for attempted murder and possible money laundering. An additional charge for murder was expected pending further investigation of the Muñoz killing.

After chaining him to a chair in an interrogation room, Rosie and Vince set matching chairs across the metal table from him and started to fire questions at him regarding who the paintings were going to, what his real job was at the art gallery and why Shapiro was sending cash out of the country.

Moreno closed his eyes, remained silent throughout the interrogation and finally lowered his head. He seemed to put himself into a trance in an exaggerated attempt to filter out the noise.

Finally, in slow motion, he opened his eyes and lifted his head until he stared at the opposite wall. With equal deliberation, he said, "I want a lawyer, but not just *any* lawyer. I want Sandy Dunn to represent me—*now*!"

Rosie stood and took a step back. "We can't do that. It'll blow the case."

Moreno twisted in his seat and the chains securing him to the metal chair rattled. He clenched his jaw at the sound. "I want my lawyer *now*."

Vince shook his head. "That's not going to happen, pal. She's involved in this case and was twice a victim: once when you kidnapped her and then . . . well, when you saved her life."

Moreno glared from one detective to the other but remained silent.

Rosie laughed. "You're a piece of work, my friend. First you assault and kidnap the victim and then you save her life? Why?"

Moreno looked directly at Rosie, his face taking on a more serene look. "Why what?"

Rosie turned to Vince, gave him a look of frustration, and focused again on the suspect. "First, why did you shoot Seth Shapiro? You said it was to save Ms. Dunn—but why? And why do you think she'd even consider representing you when you're involved somehow in her near-death experience?"

"I want to see her. I'll tell you everything but first let me talk to Sandra Dunn."

"Good luck with that," Vince said with a chuckle. "You think she'd agree to talk to you after what you've put her through?"

Moreno gave Vince a sneer. "I saved her life. She owes me. The least she could do is see me."

"You want her to thank you for shooting Shapiro?" Vince asked wide-eyed.

"You got this all wrong." A vein pulsed on one side of Moreno's forehead. He spat onto the floor, tried to wipe his mouth but the chains stopped his hands midway up. "I have to explain things to her. Tell her to talk to her mom first. She'll see me after that."

Rosie turned to Vince. "This case keeps getting crazier all the time, but now I'm curious. I'll talk to Dunn. You try to get this creep to tell you where all that money in the paintings came from."

Moreno shook his head and closed his eyes again. "No more talkin'! Not another word until I've seen Sandy. Tell her it's important."

"Fine! Come on, Vince. You're with me. Seems the only way we'll get answers is to have Dunn meet with this guy."

The paramedics had examined Sandy at the crime scene and determined that she was not harmed. The detectives questioned her briefly about why she had gone to the gallery, but she seemed too upset to say much so they had a uniformed officer take her home. She agreed that she needed to rest and time to digest all that had happened.

When Vince called her to explain Angel Moreno's request, her first reaction was, "I don't want anything to do with that man, and anyway that would jeopardize the case against him. Me, as his victim, decide to defend him? That's ridiculous!"

"I get that. However, Detective Young and I can't figure out why he shot his boss to save you. There's something else going on here that we're not seeing and Moreno's not saying anything until he talks to you. Do you have any idea what he wants?"

"Detective, I'm as confused as you are. I've dealt with men like that before. They don't sacrifice their freedom to save the victim. Those men had you and your partner cornered. It was the police against them and I couldn't tell who was going to win. What I was pretty sure of was that I was going to die in the process."

"We wouldn't have let that happen," Vince said.

"I appreciate that, but you didn't see what Moreno did before he shot Shapiro. He looked at me—*directly at me*—and grabbed for his gun. I was sure he was going to kill me. When the gun fired . . . well, let's say I was surprised that Shapiro went down instead of me."

"Sandy, why were you even at the gallery tonight?"

"Unfortunately, that comes under the heading of attorney-client privilege."

"Sandy, Shapiro could have killed you tonight. Is it worth it to hide behind misplaced ethics?" Vince asked.

Sandy grew pensive for a moment before she admitted, "He asked me to stop by for a consultation, said he needed my advice on a legal matter. He told me he didn't want to discuss it by phone."

"Did he sound angry with you when he called?"

"No, and he didn't mention anything about killing me, if that's what you're asking."

"Angel Moreno prevented that from happening. Do you know why?"

"Honestly, Detective, I'm so confused right now, I don't know what to think."

"That's what we need to know. Why did Moreno shoot Shapiro instead of you? There's a backstory here and we're missing it. I think Moreno knows what that is and that's why he saved your life. Talk to your mother. Moreno seems to think that she'll convince you to talk to him, but he won't say why."

"Detective, I absolutely have no clue why he thinks my mother could sway me to visit with him. He's the person who assaulted me. Why would she want me to have anything to do with him?"

"Sandy, do me a favor and speak with your mom. Whatever Moreno wants to see you about, we think it somehow involves your mother."

"That's insane. My mother is the most law-abiding citizen I know. She doesn't know or deal with criminals—now or ever!"

"I understand that, but Moreno won't speak to us until he sees you and that means you have to be convinced to do that—and he thinks your mother will help you see that."

"I guess I have little choice in the matter. The attorney in me has this drive to dig for the truth. In all honesty, though, there's a part of me that wants to hide under the bed. I don't know what my mother has to do with any of this, but I have a feeling I won't like the answer when I ask her." She looked down, gripped the phone tighter and shook her head. "I'll talk to her. After that, I'll call you with my decision."

Sandy hung up the phone and immediately drove to her mother's house, a middle-class ranch-style in a quiet subdivision not far from Sandy's apartment. As Sandy turned down the familiar street where she grew up, she bit her lip and pulled over to the curb. She observed how tall the trees had grown since she'd lived in the neighborhood and marveled that she'd never noticed that before.

She thought back to the day they moved in, on Sandy's fifth birthday, and how happy her mother had been that day. Her mother often told her about how proud she was to live in such a safe neighborhood since it was just the two of them. Although her mother worked hard as a legal assistant to a busy attorney, money was tight and home ownership was a distant dream until an unexpected inheritance from her parents came literally knocking at their door.

Sandy remembered how sad her mother had been when her parents died, one within a few months of the other, but how grateful she was when a lawyer knocked at the door to the apartment they were living in and announced that her parents—Sandy's grandparents—had left a sizeable inheritance in her mother's name. Although the windfall came as a shock, her mother soon understood that it would buy a safe existence for both of them and provide an abundant educational fund for her child.

The memories of her childhood and the good times playing in the neighborhood gave Sandy the courage to involve her mother in a case that neither of them had any business getting into the middle of. She drove the rest of the way to the house and parked in the driveway.

After ringing the doorbell, it took only a few moments for her mother to answer it. As she did, she smiled at Sandy and gave her a big hug before escorting her to the living room. "Sandy, what a pleasant, unexpected surprise . . . but . . . what are you doing here on a workday?"

"Mom, something happened last night. I was at a client's business and there was a shooting."

Dolores Dunn stood back and studied her daughter's face before looking her up and down. "Were you hurt? Why didn't you call?"

"No, I'm fine, Mom. I didn't want to worry you needlessly and it was late. But there's a problem with the case and I need your help."

"My help—with a shooting? Isn't that your area of expertise?"

Sandy sat on the couch, took a deep breath and willed her hands to stop fidgeting. She looked at the grandfather clock in the corner of the room and remembered how she loved to play in front of it. She'd wait for it to chime the hour with its rich, musical tones.

She turned to her mother and patted the cushion next to her on the couch. "Mom, please sit. I need to ask you some questions."

With a frown on her face, Dolores tucked a stray strand of hair behind her ear and settled onto the couch. She smoothed down her dress before turning to her daughter. "What's going on?"

"Mom, do you know a man named Angel Moreno?"

Her mother gasped as if someone had slapped her across the face. She seemed to suddenly become short of breath and drew a hand to her throat. "Where did you hear that name?"

"Mom, do you know this person?" When her mother remained silent, Sandy persisted. "It's a simple question, Mom. Do you know this person or not?"

Dolores put a shaky finger to her mouth and chewed on a cuticle for a moment. The only noise came from a passing car moving down the street until, as if on cue, the clock chimed the hour and began its musical litany.

Sandy smiled and closed her eyes. "Remember how I used to play on the floor near that clock and wait for the hour to chime? I'd lie on my back and wave my hands pretending to conduct an orchestra."

"Yes, I remember. Sometimes I wish you were that little girl again. You were such a happy child." Dolores reached up and touched Sandy's cheek delicately. "There's something I should have told you a long time ago. I hope you'll forgive me."

"Mom, what is it?" Sandy studied her mother's face. She saw only anguish and moisture threatened to spill from eyes that seemed fearful. She touched her mother's hand and gave it a squeeze. "It's okay, Mom. Whatever it is, I'm all grown up now. I can handle whatever you say."

"This man . . . this criminal . . . he wasn't always that way."

"So you know this man? When? How?"

With a quivering lip, Dolores blurted out, "He's your father!"

Sandy stood. "What?" She walked to the other side of the room and turned around. "My father? You told me he died in a car accident before I was born. That was a lie?"

"I couldn't have anything to do with him."

"Well, he got you pregnant, so he was in your life at some point—or did he . . ."

"No, nothing like that. I loved him so much at the time. He was wonderful to me . . . but he . . . he walked out of my life and I realized what a fool I had been. I didn't realize until much later what he really was."

"That he was a criminal? He's a murderer! When did you find out?"

"Much later, years after you were born. I worked for a successful attorney. You know how it is. I had access to investigators—people I trusted and who became my friends. They did special favors for me."

"Why did you try to find him? Did you still love him?"

"Yes . . . no . . . maybe both. I don't know and now I don't really care. At the time I needed to know something about him."

Sandy returned to the couch, sat and reached out for her mother's hand. "What did you learn? Did whatever you discover about him give you peace, provide some closure?"

Her mother's face scrunched up into a grimace before exploding into a soft cry and finally sobs. Sandy hugged her mother until both could speak again. Dolores shook her head side to side. "It confirmed what I was already thinking."

"Which was what? That my father was in a drug gang and a murderer?"

"Well, yes, that too. But the investigators confirmed where the money came from."

Sandy took Dolores by the shoulders and held her at arms length. "What money?"

"The inheritance from my parents—the money that never really came from them."

Sandy looked to the side and out the front window to the house across the street. An older gentleman, the present owner, was weeding a flowerbed near the porch. He waved to a passerby as he continued puttering in the garden. Sandy took a moment to think before focusing on her mother again.

"You mean the money you supposedly inherited from Grandpa—the money that bought this house and paid for my education?"

Dolores responded by sobbing louder. "I'm . . . so . . . sorry." When she reeled in her emotions, she told Sandy, "I thought about giving the money back, but it was too late. This house, law school for you—what was the point?"

"Mom, the point is I'm a lawyer now because of drug money. Revenue from criminal activity sent me to law school. I don't know what to think about that."

Her mother shook her head and mumbled, "Neither did I."

It took three more hours before Sandy called Vince back. She told him, "Detective, I'm ready to meet with Angel Moreno."

"What did your mother say to convince you?"

"It's complicated. I'll be at the station within the hour. My mother's coming with me."

"Does she know this guy?"

"She helped me understand a few things."

There was a moment of silence. Vince asked, "Sandy, are you okay?"

"I'm still on the line, Detective. I think . . . I'll explain later, but it's time for me to confront Angel Moreno."

Chapter 20

When Sandy and her mother arrived at the police station, both were red-eyed. Blotchy cheeks showed where makeup had been wiped from their faces. Dolores looked worried. Sandy was focused—a hardened, determined look on her face.

Sandy gazed down the long corridor, waited until a couple of policemen in uniform walked past, and guided her mother down the hall toward the detectives waiting outside an interrogation room. As they approached the detectives, Sandy said, "Please, no questions now. After I meet with Moreno, I'll tell you what I can. Hopefully, he'll give us the information to close your murder cases."

"Vince called the DEA." Rosie glanced toward Dolores. "They wanted specifics. We didn't have much except that Moreno said he was meeting a plane at Stinson Municipal to hand off the paintings—and the money. We intercepted a private jet that landed there. The pilot had filed a flight plan that continued to Columbia."

"Can you stay with my mother while I visit with him?" Sandy asked Rosie.

"Sure. Vince will take you in."

Vince stepped forward and rubbed his hands together. He looked around the crowded corridor before guiding Sandy to one side. "We sort of stretched the truth, told the DEA we had proof that the pilot was about to transport drug money. They grounded the plane and took the paintings into evidence, but . . . we need much more before they can make a case."

Sandy glanced toward the door to the interrogation room. "I hope I'll have more details soon." She stepped further down the hallway and motioned for Vince to follow.

"What did your mother tell you?" he asked.

"I'm asking politely. Please leave her out of this for now. She doesn't have answers, only speculation and suspicion—bits and pieces really." Sandy looked again at the door she was about to enter. She swallowed hard. "I'll have a clearer picture of what we're dealing with after I visit with him."

Vince nodded and escorted her into the interrogation room. Settling into a chair opposite Moreno, she glanced at the dull gray walls and the starkness of the room before focusing on Moreno. His feet were chained to the floor, his hands cuffed and attached to his feet by a short extension that allowed for minimal hand movements. He gave her a gentle smile.

Sandy turned to Vince. "We'll need some privacy and . . . I need a favor. Turn off the recording equipment and the speaker to this room. I'm declaring that I'm this man's attorney of record from this moment forward and I want everything we say to remain confidential."

Vince frowned and his face tightened into a worried look.

"I'll be fine, Detective," Sandy said. "This man saved my life before. He won't harm me now. A little privacy, please?"

When Vince left the room and closed the door, she turned to Moreno. The pleasant expression she maintained for the detective was replaced by a look of disgust. She leaned in closer to the man, stared into his eyes. "So you're my father?"

Moreno's lower lip quivered. He pulled at the chains and his arm muscles knotted. He lowered his gaze, as if embarrassed at the emotion he seemed unable to control.

Sandy stared at him, studied his face and paid closer attention to his features. She held her gaze a little longer on his nose and mouth. It seemed familiar, like looking into a mirror. Moreno lowered his head, brought cuffed hands to his face. He wiped moisture from his eyes and jutted out his chin. It took several more seconds before he spoke.

"Your mother . . . we were just kids, but I loved her. Her mom and dad . . . they tried to keep us apart. I was kind of wild—crazy wild at times—I could have killed them for that."

"She said you two were about to run away. Instead you left without her."

He clenched his fists. "Years later I found her, tried to explain how stupid that was."

Sandy looked down. The floor under the table was scuffed with black heel marks from past occupants. "'Too late to fix anything', my mother said."

"I know she's still pissed, but I had to leave. It . . . I couldn't handle it. It got complicated."

"The complicated part is what you did to me—and to Mr. Mason. You *did* do that?"

"No . . . Muñoz did that. I only set it up, but I made sure he didn't hurt you when he did."

"What? You used Muñoz to do your dirty work, then you killed him?"

Moreno remained silent. He shook his head to flick back strands of greasy hair that had fallen across his forehead. He stared at a blank wall.

Sandy smirked. "No answer for that? How about this? If you loved my mother and me, why did you almost have me killed?"

"To protect you! Don't you get that?"

"No, I *don't*. It makes no sense."

"Seth Shapiro thought you were beginning to understand what his real business was, that you were suspicious of all the paintings being sent to Columbia."

"You mean Mr. Mason's paintings? I have no idea what you're talking about, but my mother thinks it has to do with drugs. Is she right?"

Moreno's back stiffened. He sat straighter. His jaw muscles tightened and released. "You really didn't know?"

"Know what?" she demanded.

"Shapiro thought you knew that he was laundering money for a Mexican cartel, that he was taking a big cut and sending the rest to Columbia to pay for more drug shipments to Mexico."

Sandy's fingers touched her lips. "He what? I suspected something was going on that he wasn't telling me. He started to treat me differently, like he was unhappy with me as his attorney. When I asked if everything was okay, he shrugged it off as nothing."

"Shapiro thought you were going to confront Mason to find out if he was involved."

"I knew nothing about this, never suspected that Mason's paintings were being used to smuggle money."

"He thought you knew, wanted me to silence both of you. At first he thought about killing you and Mason, but . . . you see . . . in the past . . ."

"You've killed before, I assume?"

"That's why I left without your mother so long ago. I got mixed up in a Mexican drug gang. She would have been dragged into it. I had to leave to protect her."

"Shapiro asked you to kill me and Mr. Mason?"

"That was his first thought, but soon he realized that he wanted to keep you as his lawyer—he knew how good you were. He needed a good lawyer on his side."

"And what about Gerry Mason?"

"He needed Mason to keep painting and Mason was good at keeping to the schedule. He asked me to figure out a way to keep both of you from talking."

"But we didn't know—at least I didn't—about Shapiro's real business. He wanted to kill us because of what he *thought we knew*?"

Moreno gave her a pleading look. "I would *never* have done that, not to you. And if

Mason had gotten killed, you'd get suspicious. So I came up with a different plan."

Looking down, he gripped the table with cuffed hands. "While in Mexico, I learned a lot about drugs and cartels, *and* how to do unspeakable things to people. I met Muñoz and he taught me so much . . . how to control people, to play with their minds in ways you can't imagine."

"Hypnosis and computer chips too?"

He shrugged. "It was . . . fun, a thrill. Only Muñoz was so much better. He used to help out in the prison's drug dispensary and learned a lot about drugs."

She folded both arms across her chest. "So you had him do what you couldn't do?"

"He knew how to figure out the doses. He used to read all kinds of medical books in the dispensary. The warden found out and assigned him to kitchen duty instead. That's where I met Muñoz."

So he was the one who injected Mr. Mason and me? He figured out how much to give that almost but didn't really kill us?"

"I might have killed you by mistake if I had filled that dart and given the injection myself."

"So the dart to initially tranquilize me and the sedatives after the hypnosis could have killed me if you got the dosing slightly wrong? And the same with Mr. Mason?"

"Yeah, and I couldn't take the chance. That's why I had Muñoz do it. He was so good at guessing people's weight and fixing the right dose. He was always right on the money."

"When you both did this in the past—after getting out of prison?"

Moreno jutted out his chin and looked away before he nodded.

Sandy's upper lip curled and she swallowed hard. She leaned forward in her chair, placed her hands flat on the table in front of her. "The police tell me Muñoz was murdered. Is that because of you?"

Moreno avoided her gaze and mumbled, "I had to. He'd served his purpose."

When he glanced her way, Sandy raised an eyebrow, squared her jaw and stared right back at him. He looked down and sniggered softly. "I was so cocky. Shapiro knew what he had in me. That's how I became his right-hand man. I did whatever he needed . . . but I couldn't do that to you. I found another way to control you, to protect you—Mason also. I had to include him so you wouldn't dig into his death."

She folded her arms to prevent her hands from trembling. "I can see how you thought that would work. What I still don't understand is how Shapiro's money laundering works. He takes money from Mexican cartels and gives it to Columbian drug dealers?"

"The cartels make so much money on drug distribution into the States. They have to launder it somehow. They needed a go-between with the drug makers so there'd be no connection between them."

Sandy held up a hand. "Okay, I get it. Shapiro takes the Mexican cartels' money, more than one cartel I take it, draws off a big chunk for himself and passes the rest to the Columbians to buy more drugs. And you help him do this?"

Moreno sat back in his chair, a look of embarrassment on his face. "Sure, that's about it."

"So how do these drugs bought with laundered money get from South America to Mexico?"

He furrowed his brow and shrugged. "I don't know. It's a whole other thing. We controlled our part and didn't worry about the rest. I guess others did their thing. I know keeping everything separate protects the cartel bosses."

"You *do* know that all of this has to come out. The police are getting the DEA involved. There's no way I can protect you from prosecution, nor would I want to."

Moreno clenched and unclenched his hands. The chains rattled against the table edge. "I'm not asking you to protect me. I'm ready to pay for what I did. I want to protect *you* from getting into this . . . from *you* becoming a victim again in Shapiro's crappy scheme."

Sandy closed her eyes and lifted a hand to her forehead. "I'm still confused." She looked directly at her father. "Why put Mason and me into a coma overnight? Why not just hypnotize us to forget about the shipments—which, as it turns out, we never knew about anyway?"

"That was Muñoz's idea. He loved to play with his victims. He said we'd scare the hell out of both of you by having you subconsciously remember that if you ever said anything about the shipments, then you'd really die the next time. He said that sort of hypnosis would work. He researched it for weeks before we attacked you."

"You mean both Mason and me."

"No, I only went when Muñoz attacked you. I would've killed him if he had hurt you. Mason . . . not so much."

Sandy nodded and took in a deep breath, let it escape slowly from her mouth and stared into her father's eyes. "Somehow, I believe that. I even forgive you, considering that you saved my life—not once, but twice."

"That's all I ask—that you know the truth. I couldn't sacrifice you. I need you and your mother to understand that. I also want her to know why I left her. It might have been different if I'd known about you."

She frowned. "My mother didn't tell you that she was pregnant?"

"Not until I tried to contact her years later. I searched and found her. I went to your house and saw you playing in the front yard. You were so cute in your pink dress. I walked up and that's when your mother came to the door." Moreno closed his eyes, as if remembering the moment. He looked up at the ceiling and shook his head. "She looked like she'd seen a ghost. She glanced at me and in a second ran to you, picked you up and held you tight until she put you down on the porch. It ripped my heart out."

"What did she say?"

"She said one thing. 'Go away and never come back' and threw a rock at me, gashed the side of my face." He bowed his head. "I never went back."

"My mother thinks you're involved in drug activity. Why would she know that?"

"I got mixed up in drug dealing, started when I was a kid. That's why your mother and I were going away, to run from that life and our parents. She wanted me to start over."

Sandy tilted her head, a questioning frown on her forehead. "You left without her, though."

"Some little shit found out I was trying to get out. He told the drug boss. The guy would have killed both of us before letting me go. I had no choice but to stay."

"What drug boss—who were you working for?"

"Doesn't matter now. It's done."

Sandy stared at Moreno for a moment before nodding that she understood. "My mother told me that you died in a car accident before I was born. She described my dad as someone quite different from you. How are you so sure you're really my father?"

"I did a DNA test on a glass you used at Shapiro's office, had it tested against mine to be sure. I'm your father." Moreno put his hands together, resting them on the table's surface. The chains rattled again. "I followed your life from a distance. I knew that your mom's parents had died and left her a comfortable inheritance."

"You bastard. I know all about how you set her up to take drug money." She stood and raised a hand to slap him. He flinched and that stopped her. "Think you're so smart? Paying her off to sooth your conscience?"

"What? No, I wanted to provide a good life for you."

Sandy raked fingers through her hair. "What you did was make my mother an accessory to money laundering. She took that money and bought a house, provided a great education for me, paid for law school even."

"Yeah, so?"

She threw up her hands. "So, I'm the product of the cartels. My whole life was bought with drug money. I'm a success because others have overdosed—died—to make that happen. Do you have any idea what kind of ethical position that puts me in?"

"Who's to know? I'll never tell."

Sandy put hands on her hips and chuckled. "Sounds about right. Did Shapiro know about me being your daughter?"

"Of course not. I couldn't believe, though, that he hired you—*my daughter*—to be his attorney. I couldn't stop him. He'd get suspicious and you'd be a liability that he'd have to get rid of right away."

Sandy pursed her lips together and looked up at the stained ceiling for a moment before staring back at him. "I can't represent you. I can't get you out of this mess. You'll need someone much better than me to help you now."

"I understand that, but I want you to represent me only to get a better deal than at trial. I owe you the right to put me behind bars, but I don't want to be locked away forever for trying to do the right thing."

She squared her shoulders, set her jaw and pointed at him. "The deal is you have to tell the truth, for my sake as well as my mother's. You have to testify against Seth Shapiro and against his Mexican and Columbian connections. You have to say that Mr. Mason knew nothing about how his paintings were involved in money laundering. You have to make this right for him. He's another victim."

Moreno nodded but remained silent.

Sandy stood and turned toward the door.

"You know they'll kill me before this even goes to trial," Moreno blurted out.

She spun around. "Who will?"

Take your pick—the Mexicans or the Columbians. I'm dead either way."

"That won't happen. The police will protect you."

He laughed. "Don't be so sure of that."

She sat back down, reached out and laid a hand over his. "I'll do whatever I can to protect you, but in the end you'll have to take responsibility for what you did. And you'll need an attorney with better experience than I have to help you through this."

He nodded his agreement.

She stood, turned to walk out, but glanced back. "I need your permission help your new attorney work out a deal. You have to tell those detectives and the DEA everything. Shapiro is in the hospital now, but he belongs in jail for a very long time. Will you help me make that happen?"

"Do whatever you have to. I'll cooperate."

Without saying another word, she turned the door handle and slipped out of the room. She walked over to the detectives who were sitting on a hallway bench on either side of her mother. She glanced from one to the other. "I have a lot to explain and so does the man sitting in that room."

Rosie nodded and stood. "Then we'd better get started."

Sandy's mother looked up at her daughter. "What did Angel tell you? Was I right about him?"

"Mom, please. Let me handle this."

Sandy clasped her hands together and straightened her back. She glanced toward Rosie. "I'm about to give you access to valuable information that will be of great interest to the DEA and it will also solve your murder cases. But first I'm going to need your cooperation."

"Go on," said Rosie cautiously. Vince only rubbed his chin and nodded.

Sandy gave the detectives an awkward grin. "That man in there is my father."

Her mother pleaded, "Sandy, don't."

The detectives glanced from daughter to mother and then looked at each other wide-eyed. Words seem to fail them.

Sandy continued. "I'm not sure how I feel about that, and there are . . . complications, but he says he's ready to talk and take responsibility for his actions." She turned to her mother. "That includes him acting like a father."

"It'll be a cold day in hell," her mother said.

"Mother, please. Just hear me out." Sandy turned to the detectives. "Before anything else, I'm going to get him a more qualified lawyer. If you'll consider dealing with him for what information he can offer and protect him from his enemies, I think you'll find him very cooperative."

Rosie raised a hand. "Okay, this is a lot to digest at once, but you have my word that we'll work with him if he has information that puts key drug dealers and murderers away."

"I appreciate that, Detective, and I'll have to convince the DEA to do the same."

Rosie nodded. "I can almost bet that the DEA will agree to that if Moreno helps put the right people behind bars."

Sandy turned to her mother and smiled. "It's really going to be alright, Mom. We have a long way to go, but we'll work through this together—all of us."

Acknowledgements:

First and foremost, I thank my wife Ginger for her continued encouragement of my writing career and for her eternal patience when I forget to balance my writing with the rest of my life.

To my friends at ALIR, I give special thanks for helping me work through the initial drafts of this novel. ALIR— the Academy of Learning in Retirement—provides lifelong learning and enrichment in a variety of subjects to the older adult. Talented volunteers share their wealth of experience and expertise with fellow members in a classroom setting.

A special *Thank You* goes to our class moderator, Jean Jackson. Her cultivation of writers and her dedication to teaching the art of writing has inspired not only me but the many who are and were fortunate enough to be part of her class.

I am grateful to be included in this group of supportive writers who share a passion for the written word. My ALIR family, under the direction of Jean Jackson, played a large role in helping me evolve my idea from a short story into this full novel.

To my Facebook, Twitter and blog fans, I am thankful for your support and continued promotion of my weekly "Prescription For Murder" blog. I truly appreciate all of you.

Finally, I give a most important "Thank You" to my readers for allowing me to share some of my Murder, Mayhem and Medicine with you.

James J. Murray
August 29, 2016

A Message from James J. Murray

Thank you for reading ***Almost Dead***. I hope you enjoyed the book as much as I enjoyed writing it.

It all started with a writing critique class that I attend regularly. One day I promised to bring in about ten pages of a work in progress for the next class. I thought I'd start a new short story about a couple of victims who mysteriously died but woke up and resumed their normal activity the next day. I wrote the first chapter and read it at the next class meeting. Everyone liked it—a lot—and asked for more. I was thrilled and went home to further develop the plot.

Soon I realized that the storyline could not be resolved in the length of a normal short story, so I re-outlined the plot into a novella. As the story unfolded, however, I discovered that the characters could not be contained in anything less than a novel-length story and continued to write it to completion.

The members of that critique class eventually read the entire novel piece-by-piece. Based on their suggestions, there have been tweaks here and there before the novel went to my editor. I've dedicated the novel to that critique class.

If you liked this story, please take a moment to let my readers know that by rating it and posting a review: http://www.amazon.com/dp/B01AEU2RAG
Or
https://www.goodreads.com/book/show/28690346-almost-dead
It will only take a moment and I would truly appreciate it.

About The Author

JAMES HAS EXPERIENCE IN BOTH PHARMACEUTICAL MANUFACTURING AND CLINICAL PATIENT MANAGEMENT. MEDICATIONS AND THEIR IMPACT ON A PATIENT'S QUALITY OF LIFE HAS BEEN HIS EXPERTISE.

HIS SECRET PASSION OF MURDER AND MAYHEM, HOWEVER, IS A WHOLE OTHER MATTER. AN OBSESSION WITH READING MURDER MYSTERIES AND THRILLERS LEFT HIM LONGING TO WEAVE SUCH TALES OF HIS OWN.

DRAWING ON PAST CLINICAL EXPERTISE AS A PHARMACIST AND AN INFATUATION WITH THE LETHAL EFFECTS OF DRUGS, JAMES CREATES SHORT STORIES AND NOVELS THAT WILL HAVE YOU LOOKING OVER YOUR SHOULDER AND SUSPICIOUS OF ANYTHING IN YOUR MEDICINE CABINET. JAMES LIVES IN SOUTH TEXAS WITH HIS WIFE AND THREE CATS.

JAMES WRITES A WEEKLY BLOG CALLED "PRESCRIPTION FOR MURDER" THAT HIGHLIGHTS THE MANY LETHAL SUBSTANCES USED AS MURDER WEAPONS IN MODERN FICTION. FOR AN INTERESTING READ AND TO LEARN ABOUT HIS LATEST PUBLICATIONS, SUBSCRIBE TO HIS BLOG.

Website:

http://www.jamesjmurray.com/
Blog:
https://jamesjmurray.wordpress.com/
Facebook:
https://www.facebook.com/jamesjmurraywriter/
Twitter:
https://twitter.com/JamesJMurray1
Amazon Author Page:
www.amazon.com/author/jamesjmurray
Goodreads Author Page:
www.goodreads.com/jamesjmurray

A Preview of *Lethal Medicine*

By James J. Murray

As a bonus, I've included the first two chapters of my full-length novel ***Lethal Medicine***. It was first published in 2015 and has received numerous five-star reviews. It was re-published in 2016 with updated cover art.

The sequel, called ***Imperfect Murder***, is scheduled for release in late Fall 2016.

Lethal Medicine

Detectives Rosie Young and Vince Mendez solve a case in which Jon Masters, a clinical pharmacist, becomes the victim of an elaborate scheme to redefine the nation's recreational drug culture when evidence found at a crime scene implicates Jon in drug trafficking and murder. Jon races against time, eventually with the help of a trusted friend from his days in Special Forces, to uncover an international conspiracy.

****

SAN ANTONIO, TEXAS

~ 1 ~

"What a way to start the day!" Rosie said to her partner. "A total waste of time."

"Only one way to find out," Vince said as they arrived at the Bexar County Medical Examiner's Office located on the sprawling campus of The University of Texas Health Science Center.

They checked in at the reception desk. "I'm Homicide Detective Rosie Young and this is my partner Vince Mendez," she announced. Like many in San Antonio, Rosie was of

Mexican descent, her last name a carryover from a failed marriage that ended three years previously. She was dressed in her usual detective attire—a pair of starched black jeans, a brightly colored tank top and a short black jacket. She had been a police officer for twelve years and a homicide detective for four.

"We're here to follow-up on the autopsy of Jessica Arredondo," she said.

The receptionist nodded and pulled out a three-ring binder. "Sure, let me check my log. Yes, Arredondo, brought in two nights ago . . . that would be Dr. Rebecca Nolan. Her office is through the main doors, down the hall, and—"

Rosie interrupted, held up a hand. "We know where Becky is. You're new here?"

"Second day, I'll buzz you in."

Vince Mendez—her partner—a nine-year veteran of the police force and two years as a homicide detective, walked a couple of lengths behind Rosie. Arriving at Dr. Nolan's office, they found her deep in conversation.

When she noticed the detectives, Nolan said, "Come on in. There's someone I want you to meet. Detectives Rosie Young and Vince Mendez, this is DEA Special Agent Brian Vargas. Agent Vargas, these are the two homicide detectives assigned to the Arredondo case."

The detectives and the DEA agent shook hands, mumbled greetings to each other and followed the medical examiner to the autopsy pit.

Nolan noted the detectives' perplexed expressions. "I asked Agent Vargas to join us. I have a preliminary tox screen from the blood I took at the scene and found an interesting coincidence."

"I'm all ears," Rosie said. "But I don't understand why the DEA is here on a probable overdose case, or even why you called us in. What's so special about this one?"

"I'll explain that shortly. Trust me for now that Agent Vargas should hear this also." They walked up to the table that held Jessica Arredondo. Becky pulled back the sheet covering the body. "I found no trace to link the delivery boy to the victim. That's consistent with samples taken from his clothing and fingernails by the forensic techs, no transfer from her or the bed."

"Boy? What boy?" Agent Vargas asked.

"Jason Hanson," Vince said. "He was delivering Chinese take-out down the hall and noticed the victim's apartment door ajar. When he finished his delivery, he walked back past and saw it was still open. He alerted the lobby security guard as he was leaving the building."

"Upscale apartment building," Vargas commented.

"One of the nice ones popping up on the northern edge of the city—great views of the foothills to the north. Anyway, the guard thought it best to hold on to Jason and together they checked out the situation. They eventually went to the bedroom and discovered the body."

Nolan picked up the dead woman's right hand. "I found skin under her nails. I tested that against the DNA sample from the boy and there's no match. I'd say he's not involved.

"What do you think, detectives?" Vargas asked.

Vince shrugged. "That was one scared kid but it could have been an act."

"If he was acting, I'd give him an award," Rosie added.

The DEA agent frowned. "So what's the story on the victim?"

"No ID in her purse and no credit cards but over a hundred in cash. The guard said her name is Jessica Arredondo, but pictures in the bedroom identify her as 'Just Jess'."

"You mean photos of her with captions?" Vargas asked.

"More like promotional photos, like she was promoting herself as being all someone needs," Vince said with a chuckle. Always ready with a wisecrack, Rosie had learned quickly to look past that and beyond Vince's lanky frame and ill-fitting suits. The sports jacket he had on was too short over his narrow torso. His wrists poked out from the ends of the sleeves. True, the man couldn't dress himself but he could solve any case he put his mind to.

Rosie explained. "There was a stack of glamour photos on the dresser and that's how she signed them. And we found other . . . things too."

"What other things?" Vargas asked.

"Some interesting leather things for starters. Sexy lingerie. Expensive clothes. That sort of stuff."

Vince glanced at Vargas and gave a wry smile. "We also found some curious toys."

Rosie glared at Vince before turning back to Vargas. "And we found lots of other cash, thousands in a drawer."

Vargas rubbed a hand across his forehead. "A hooker?"

Vince nodded. "And an expensive one at that."

"Regarding the victim," Nolan said after clearing her throat. "Based on liver temp and degree of rigor, she'd been dead for about four hours." Although Nolan was in her late thirties, she looked ten years younger. It was only her careful attention to detail that made people take notice and respect her as a serious scientist.

"She died of a massive intravenous overdose of heroin. I personally checked around the crime scene that night for any drug paraphernalia. There was none. I'd say the drug was not self-administered. She was murdered."

"Isn't that a leap, Becky?" Vince asked. "Couldn't she have disposed of the syringe after injecting herself? Maybe she flushed it down the toilet before going back to bed."

"I thought of that, but it doesn't explain what happened. She had about five times the lethal dose of heroin in her body." Becky pushed back some of her red hair that had fallen over one eye and walked closer to the body. "She wouldn't have had time to inject the drug, dispose of the syringe and get back to the bed. She would've become unconscious within seconds. I think she died on the bed she was found in."

Nolan lifted one of the victim's arms. "I believe whoever administered that lethal dose simply overpowered her. Some bruising showed up on her upper arms during autopsy. The skin under her nails indicates she tried to defend herself." She gently put the victim's arm down. "The lab still can't get a DNA match through the databases, though."

Rosie thought out loud. "So we have a murder and our only suspect is that kid who's just been cleared." She glanced at Agent Vargas as her hands came to rest on her hips. "And why are you here, anyway? The DEA doesn't get involved in drug murders without good reason."

Agent Vargas flashed her a smile. "Smart and pretty. What a combination!"

Rosie gave Vargas a venomous stare. "Could we continue, please?"

"Detective, there's much more involved here than simple murder. Why don't we let the ME explain and you'll see what I mean."

Turning to Nolan, Rosie asked, "Becky, what's he talking about?"

Looking from Vargas to Detective Young, Nolan said, "Alright, let's move on, shall we? Rosie, the heroin itself is the most interesting part of the case. I took a sample of some liquid I found on the victim's skin near the injection site. It probably leaked from the syringe before the needle pierced her skin. The preliminary results show it's an unusually pure heroin hydrochloride, something around 99% pure. The hydrochloride form makes it water-soluble. I've only seen that combination once before. It was in this facility."

Nolan leaned back to a cart and picked up a report folder from it. "Not long ago I had a case that I ruled an accidental overdose. The only significant aspects of that case were the purity of the heroin and the fact that it was the water-soluble hydrochloride kind. You and Vince were assigned to investigate until I ruled it accidental."

"I recall the case," Rosie said. "The victim's name was Nathan Wheeler. We found the heroin in a squeeze bottle that looked like a nasal spray container. You said the bottle was significant because of the heroin's chemical makeup and said that it was perfect for snorting."

Nolan pointed to Rosie and grinned. "I also documented that I thought we were seeing the beginnings of a whole new heroin distribution idea. Although I think Ms. Arredondo died of a massive heroin injection, she definitely had nasal irritation consistent with snorting a powerful drug."

"Are these cases linked?"

"The COD in both cases is a heroin overdose and in both situations the drug was unique. I reviewed Mr. Wheeler's file this morning and I still think his overdose was self-inflicted and his death accidental. That's how the cases differ." Becky paused and put the Wheeler file back on the cart. She folded her arms and nodded. "Ms. Arredondo was definitely murdered. I've ordered a chemical assay of the heroin in both cases. I suspect they're from the same source and that's why I called in the DEA. We may be seeing a new street heroin here."

Rosie turned to Special Agent Vargas, her posture rigid and her voice crisp. "You heard the doctor. The victim was murdered. I want to make it perfectly clear that this is our case."

Refusing to be chastised, Agent Vargas spoke in a professional tone. "I appreciate your candor, Detective Young, but I hope you understand I'll need to be kept informed on the progress of your case, especially as it pertains to the drug source. Otherwise, I'll become more involved than you'd like."

Rosie tilted her head and put a hand over her heart. "You have my word. We'll be cooperative and forthcoming with the results of our murder investigation."

"Becky, there was an IV bag at the crime scene. We sent it to the lab for analysis," Vince said. "It was in the victim's closet. I may be stretching here, but I wonder if that bag contained more of that same pure heroin. Could you check on the results?"

Nolan frowned, racked fingers through her red hair. "I didn't see that listed on the investigation report but I'll find out."

"It's listed on the supplemental report because I found it early on before the forensics techs arrived. I made sure one of them dusted it for prints first before sending it off, though."

"I'll check with the lab. Describe it." Nolan grabbed a notepad and pen.

"It looked like a small plastic bag you'd see hanging from a hospital IV pole. There was only a little clear liquid left in it. Whatever it was, the label said it was from a pharmacy called The Infusion Masters. We'll check the place out once we have the analysis."

Before Becky could finish writing her notes, Agent Vargas asked, “The Infusion Masters? Is that what the label had on it?”

“Why is that important?” Rosie asked.

“This may be a coincidence, but a few weeks ago we got an anonymous call suggesting that there was illegal drug activity going on in that pharmacy. I went and checked it out myself.”

“So what did you find?” Vince asked.

“Absolutely nothing. I went over their controlled drugs and their records. I couldn’t find anything unusual.”

Rosie let out a heavy sigh. “This lead’s probably another dead end.”

“Possibly, but if anything shows up in that IV bag, I’d appreciate a call.”

“As I’ve said, Special Agent, we’re always glad to cooperate with the DEA.”

~ 2 ~

After a quick shower to wash away the grime of a five-mile run, Jon toweled off and dressed in the bathroom that separated his office from his wife’s. The daily ritual from road warrior to business professional kept him focused. He looked in the mirror, allowed a crooked smile and slowly nodded to the current version of himself.

Grabbing two cups of fresh coffee on the way, he strolled down the hall to Gwen’s office.

He put the steaming cups on her desk as she glanced up. “How was the run?”

Shrugging, he answered, “Like any other, a good hurt.” He smiled and walked around his wife’s desk.

“Mmm, you smell yummy,” she said as he kissed her cheek.

Jon turned Gwen's desk chair, pulled it closer and planted a long kiss on her lips before reluctantly sliding out of their embrace. "Much more of that and we won't get any work done today."

Jon and Gwen Masters co-owned The Infusion Masters, a specialty pharmacy practice which compounded sterile IV medications for homecare patients. With Gwen's financial skills and Jon's clinical expertise, they had grown the business from a staff of three to over one hundred employees.

"I have a meeting in Austin tomorrow morning," Jon said. "Later I'm heading to Dallas for cocktails with the marketing team. How about coming along?"

Gwen leaned back in her chair, pausing to consider. "I was planning a desk day."

"We could talk about contract pricing as we drive up . . . spend the night."

She waved an upturned hand at the papers strewn across her desk. "I could use some time away from this, but I have a three o'clock on Thursday with the intake department."

Jon reached over and touched her silky, auburn hair. "I'll get you back in time. We could even mix a little pleasure with business."

Playfully eying her husband's physique, Gwen stretched her long, lean legs toward him, used them to pull him closer. "When you talk like that, how could a girl refuse? I'll ask Nikki to make some reservations."

As Gwen was about to pick up the phone to buzz her, Nikki's voice came over the phone's intercom. "Gwen, is Jon back from his run? I can't find him anywhere."

"He's here in my office. What do you need?"

"Sorry to interrupt you guys. That DEA agent is back. He's waiting in the lobby area. He wants to see Jon right away."

Jon looked at Gwen, clearly puzzled. He leaned toward the phone. "He's here for another inspection, Nikki?"

"He won't tell me what it's about but he's acting a little creepy."

"Show him to my office and let Chip know the pharmacy might get a second visit from the DEA."

Gwen remained in her chair but gave Jon a worried look. Nikki escorted the agent down the hall and into Jon's office. Jon waited a moment before venturing to his office to greet the agent.

When Jon arrived, Nikki said, "You remember DEA Special Agent Brian Vargas from a few weeks ago?"

The agent extended a hand. "Good to see you again, Mr. Masters." The men shook hands, each giving the other a wary stare. Nikki retreated to the hallway and returned to her reception desk without looking back.

Agent Vargas' stern expression clearly showed his demeanor did not mirror the pleasantry. He was dressed almost identical to what he had worn during his first visit to the pharmacy—what Jon assumed was accepted DEA fashion—a non-descript black suit, white shirt and a forgettable patterned tie.

The agent periodically tugged at his shirt collar. During the first visit, Jon wondered if this was because he was not yet comfortable in his job. But the man's eyes, as he subtly but continually scanned his surroundings, convinced Jon that he was standing before an experienced field agent.

"Agent Vargas, please have a seat. The last time I saw you, you were rather vague. You asked to see some records, took a look at our narcotics storage area and said it was a routine visit. Since then, I've learned that the DEA doesn't do regular pharmacy inspections. Yet here you are again."

"We don't inspect unless there's cause." The agent eased into a cushioned chair. "A matter has come to our attention."

Jon raised an eyebrow, causing his forehead to crease. He slowly sat in his desk chair. "Maybe you should tell me what this is about before we go any further."

"It's quite simple." Agent Vargas glanced toward the doorway as Gwen slowly walked past Jon's office. She and the agent briefly made eye contact before he turned his attention back to Jon. "Our office received information that there might be illegal activity going on in your pharmacy."

Jon looked in the direction of the hallway but Gwen had disappeared. He placed the palms of his hands on the desktop and chuckled out the words. "That's absurd."

Agent Vargas sat perfectly straight, as if every nerve ending was firing on overdrive. "The police also found an IV bag at the scene of a murder. It had your pharmacy's label on it."

Jon sat rigid in his chair. "Which patient? I've heard nothing about a murder."

"I would like to see your narcotic inventory records."

"Our pharmacy records are accurate. There's nothing illegal happening here and I certainly know nothing about one of our patients getting murdered."

Agent Vargas gazed at his watch as he stood up. "Mr. Masters, you're wasting my time. Could I see your narcotic records now, or do we have to make this difficult?"

Annoyed, Jon stood and smoothed down his linen slacks. "I'll lead the way."

Without another word, Jon escorted Agent Vargas through the business office. They passed Nikki's desk and received a quizzical glance from her as they swept by. Gwen was nowhere in sight.

They crossed the hall to the pharmacy suite. Jon walked up to Chip and introduced him to the DEA agent. "This is Special

Agent Vargas. He's here to do an inspection of the pharmacy, our narcotic records in particular. He was here a few weeks ago. It was after you had gone for the day. It seemed to be nothing so I didn't mention it."

Chip responded with a slight frown and Jon turned to the DEA agent. "This is Carlos Brown, Chip for short, and he's the Pharmacist-In-Charge of this branch of our pharmacy business."

Chip noticed the agent's serious attitude and looked to Jon for guidance. Jon shrugged to indicate that whatever the DEA agent wanted was okay with him. Chip began, "We don't look like a normal pharmacy. Maybe a tour would—"

"Your space is set up as a sterile lab to prepare IV meds, with a warehouse for drugs and supplies, and with office areas for personnel surrounding it." He crossed his arms and gave a mocking smile. "Does that about cover it?"

Chip opened his mouth to speak but faltered.

Agent Vargas sighed. "I realize everything's delivered to the patient's home and you're not open to the public like most pharmacies. I understand the concept of an infusion pharmacy and I've been here before." He rubbed his hands together. "Now show me your narcotic records and where your controlled drugs are stored."

"No problem."

Jon remained in the pharmacy during the two-hour inspection. He pulled a few patient charts to review. He twirled his Mont Blanc pen as he read and tried to look busy. He lingered a dozen feet behind Agent Vargas as the agent flipped through file after file and inspected vial after vial of medication. The sun shone brightly though the pharmacy windows as the morning progressed to noon.

Finally, the agent completed his paperwork. He gathered his forms, turned to Jon and regarded him with a more placid expression. "There are a lot of narcotics here."

Jon gave a faint shrug but straightened his shoulders when Agent Vargas continued to stare at him. "We have hospice contracts for terminal patients. That requires us to keep a large inventory on hand."

"Do all of your patients eventually die?"

"Of course not."

Jon waited for Agent Vargas to make his point but the agent stood in place with an unwavering gaze. "We have plenty of patients who aren't terminal," Jon said a little defensively. "Post-surgical complications, bone infections and whatnot."

Agent Vargas pressed his lips together.

"Most complete their therapies and go back to normal, healthy lives." Jon decided that he was talking too much. He closed his mouth, stood taller and stared at the agent.

Agent Vargas remained silent a moment longer and finally nodded. "Your records are impressive. Each drug is accounted for and everything crosschecks."

"I know that. You obviously expected something else."

Agent Vargas' lip twitched.

"Look," Jon said. "You made a serious accusation earlier. Can we go back to my office and discuss that?"

Seeming less like a hunter going after his prey than previously, the agent nodded in agreement. They returned across the hall to Jon's office. Jon sat behind his desk and Vargas took a seat in a chair on the opposite side.

"Agent Vargas, I'm sure by now you realize that we're doing nothing illegal."

"It does appear that everything is in order."

Jon leaned forward and spread his hands over the desk. "Yet you walked in here expecting to find . . . what . . . that I'm a crook . . . or maybe a murderer?"

The agent took a moment to remove his suit jacket. He draped it across the arm of the chair. "An anonymous call to our office indicated that we should check out The Infusion Masters. He insinuated you were involved in illegal narcotics distribution. That's what stimulated my first visit."

"So it was a man. Could you trace the call?"

"We tried."

Jon felt his face grow warm. "So someone who would not identify himself called and made wild accusations and you immediately jumped to conclusions?"

Agent Vargas tugged at his shirt collar and scratched his neck. "It's our job to make sure everyone follows the law. We don't leap to spontaneous conclusions. And there's that IV bag at a murder scene with your pharmacy's name on it."

Jon held his tongue. He was dangerously close to saying something that he would regret.

"The agent who took the call is experienced," said Vargas. "He believed it was credible enough to warrant a field investigation. I came but left satisfied that all seemed normal here."

"Let me get this straight. A nameless man made outrageous statements about my company without providing any proof and went to the trouble to call from a non-traceable phone. Based on that, you show up at my doorstep and accuse me of being a criminal?"

"Well, now I'm here about a murder that involves IV drugs."

"You think I'm . . . or at least my pharmacy . . . is involved somehow?"

"I'm not at liberty to say at the moment but it appears that your pharmacy is in the clear."

"It appears so? Are you not sure after tearing through my records and upsetting my chief pharmacist? You find nothing suspicious, yet I don't think you're convinced."

"Mr. Masters, let me be perfectly clear." Agent Vargas stood. He gathered his jacket from the chair arm. "I'm satisfied that things are legit here and I'm willing to put this to rest. But if anything comes over my desk about this pharmacy again, I'll be back and you won't like it one bit."

To Order ***Lethal Medicine*** from Amazon for Kindle or to order the Print Version, go to: https://www.amazon.com/author/jamesjmurray

Made in the USA
San Bernardino, CA
30 January 2017